Adjusting Sights

Haim Sabato

ADJUSTING SIGHTS

TRANSLATED BY
Hillel Halkin

The Toby Press

Second English language Edition 2003

The Toby Press *LLC*
www.tobypress.com

The right of Haim Sabato to be identified as the author of
this work has been asserted by him in accordance with the
Copyright, Designs *&* Patents Act 1988

Originally published as *Tiyum Kavanot*

Copyright © Miskal Publishing House *&* Books in the Attic, Tel Aviv

Translation copyright © Hillel Halkin 2003

ISBN I 902881 70 2, *hardcover*

A CIP catalogue record for this title
is available from the British Library

Typeset in Garamond by Jerusalem Typesetting

Printed and bound in the United States by
Thomson-Shore Inc., Michigan

A glossary of the Hebrew terms used in this book
may be found at the end

Chapter one

A pure moon shone overhead. Not a cloud hid it from sight. It was waiting to be blessed by the People of Israel, as shy as a bride who waits to be veiled by her bridegroom before stepping under the wedding canopy. Ever since the moon said to God long ago, *The sun and I cannot rule as equals and share the same crown*, and the Creator rebuked it, saying, *Then wane and be the lesser light*, the moon has humbly accepted its fate. Whenever it shines, humbleness shines with it and gives it grace.

Row after row of *Hasidim* danced before it. The younger ones wore black gabardines, the older ones, white gowns. The gowns looked like shrouds. They reminded a man of the day of his death, that he might observe the counsel of Rabbi Akavia ben Mehalalel, who said: "Think of three things and thou will not come to sin: from where you have come, to where you will go and to Whom you owe a reckoning."

Gabardined and gowned, the *Hasidim* shut their eyes and swayed, aiming their hearts at heaven and chanting, "As I dance before

Thee but cannot touch Thee, so may our enemies dance before us and neither touch nor harm us. May dread and fear befall them!"

And they repeated:

"May dread and fear befall them!"

And a third time:

"May dread and fear befall them!"

It was the end of *Yom Kippur*. It is the custom at the end of this day for the People of Israel to sanctify the moon with a special blessing. Cleansed of all their sins, they are supposed to perform a commandment at once, before Satan, envious of their purity, could find a way to entrap them. And all the more is this so because sanctifying the moon is like playing host to God, for it is written in the sayings of the Sages, *Were Israel to do no more than greet their Father in heaven once a month at the sanctification of the moon, this would suffice*. Hence the moon is sanctified standing, as if in the presence of a king. Moreover, as God is present in joy, and joy comes from purity, and the People of Israel are pure at the end of *Yom Kippur*, having stood all day in prayer and confessed their sins and abstained from food and denied themselves the pleasures of the flesh and cast off all material things until they are likened to angels, a herald voice declares, "Go, eat your bread in joy, and drink your wine gladly, for the Lord is pleased with you."

In most synagogues, so as not to prolong the ordeal of all those fasting, especially the elderly, the ill, and women with child, the evening service is said immediately after the blast of the *shofar* that marks the end of *Yom Kippur*. As soon as the day is over, the congregants sanctify the moon and hurry home.

This was the practice in the Jerusalem neighborhood of Bayit ve-Gan. Though many of its inhabitants were pious Jews who prolonged their Sabbaths and holidays according to the strict ruling of Rabbenu Tam, they too had long been at home, the hour being close to midnight. Who, then, were the *Hasidim* awaited by the moon? They were the disciples of the Rabbi of Amshinov. Loath to part with the rapture of prayer, the Amshinov *Hasidim* lingered over it even on *Yom Kippur*, extending the holiness of the fast day into ordinary time.

I was glad to see them still dancing. I had begun to think I would have to sanctify the new moon by myself, without a *minyan*, a prayer group of ten. Where was I going to find ten men at such an hour? And most of all I was glad because the Sages had said that whoever sanctifies the new moon in joy would come to no harm in the month ahead. I was about to mention this to my friend, Dov, walking at my side, so that he could put himself in a joyous mood, when the *Hasidim* pulled us into their ranks.

"Soldiers!" they cried. "Soldiers! Go to the rabbi and he'll bless you."

They parted to make a path and we were led to the rabbi, the old Amshinover *Rebbe*. His *Hasidim* crowded around us.

We were two young soldiers, Dov and I. Our packs on our shoulders, we made our way to the rabbi. We had been together since coming to Israel, Dov from Rumania and I from Egypt. Each day we had walked from Beit Mazmil to the *Talmud Torah* in Bayit ve-Gan, Dov in his black beret and I in the brightly colored cap I was given by a woman who worked for the Jewish Agency in Milan. My family had been in transit there from Cairo, waiting for the night train to Genoa, from where we would sail to Haifa on the *Artza*.

The *Talmud Torah* in Bayit ve-Gan was next to the Amshinov synagogue—outside of which, thirteen years later, we now stood near the buses parked at our assembly point. As soon as our bus was full, an officer would take charge and we would head north to our unit.

We had studied together at the same religious high school, Dov and I. We had gone together to the same *yeshiva*, whose students divided their time between their studies and the army. We had trained in the same tank at an armored corps base in Sinai. I was the gunner. Dov was the loader.

"Crew, prepare to mount the tank! Crew, mount! Driver, sharp left! Gunner, hollow charge, two thousand meters, fire! Down a hundred, fire! Up fifty, fire! Direct hit! Direct hit, hold your fire! Loader, reload! Faster, Dov! Stop dreaming! There's no time to dream in a real war. You're already in the enemy's sights."

"Yes, sir. I'm doing my best."
The loader opened the breech.

We stood watch together on a roof in Ras Sudar. We manned its southern position, looking out over the Gulf of Suez, Dov and I.

It was a Sabbath eve. Dov had finished his watch and I had come up to relieve him. It was pitch dark. There were no stars or moon. We had just finished our basic training the month before. Every splash of a fish in the water made me jump. Dov said, "I'll stay up with you. I can't sleep anyway. We can sing Sabbath hymns. Or go over a bit of *Mishnah* by heart." I knew he knew I was afraid. He stayed with me.

In theology class we had argued together about faith, and belief in God, and Redemption. Together we had studied Rabbi Nissim of Gerona's commentary on the second chapter of *Ketubot*. Together we had read The *Maharal* of Prague's *Eternity of Israel*. And together we had parted from Dov's mother on Brazil Street in Beit Mazmil an hour before.

"War," she had said. "War! What do you know about it? *I* know. And I know no one knows when you'll be home again. No one."

As she spoke she filled a tin with homemade cookies and another with cheese pastries wrapped in foil. I knew the taste of both.

"*Ima!*" Dov said. "This isn't Rumania or World War II. Think of it as a school outing—we'll be back in a few days."

To me he said softly, "I understand how she feels. She's worried. Her whole family was killed in Europe. And she's a mother. But this is just one more glorified company maneuver. We'll be back in no time. I heard on the radio that we're already counter-attacking. The air force is knocking out the Egyptian bridgeheads on the Canal. I'm only afraid that by the time we reservists get to the Golan, the regular army will have finished the job for us."

His father put down the little book of Psalms that he was reading. He kissed it and kissed his son.

At the end of *Yom Kippur,* together we walked to the assembly point. Close to midnight we were brought to the Rabbi of Amshinov by his *Hasidim,* who were sanctifying the moon. Their rabbi, they confided, could work wonders. His blessing was worth a great deal. They stood around us, straining to hear what he would say.

The Rabbi of Amshinov clasped my hand warmly between his own two and said, looking directly at me:

"May dread and fear befall them. May dread and fear befall them. Them and not you."

We parted from him and boarded the bus. We thought we'd be back soon. During the three terrible days that followed, I kept seeing the Rabbi of Amshinov before me. I kept hearing his words. Each time fear threatened to overcome me, I pictured him saying, "Them and not you. Them and not you." That calmed me.

Until I heard of Dov's death.

After that the old man stopped appearing.

The months went by. In late spring we hosed down our tanks a last time, handed in our gear, took off our uniforms, and returned to the Talmud—to the tractate of Bava Batra and the property laws of pits, cisterns, caves, olive presses, and fields. I kept meaning to go to the Rabbi of Amshinov and tell him what had happened to us after he blessed us. I wanted to tell him how our tanks were knocked out in Nafah quarry on the second day of the war, and how they burst into flames one by one, and how the blackened loader of 2-B hit the ground with his leg on fire and rolled there dowsing it with a jerry can of water. And how our tank commander, Gidi, shouted, "Gunner, fire!" and I shouted back, "I don't know what to aim at!"

"Fire, gunner! Fire at anything! We're being shot at! We're hit! Abandon tank!"

And how Roni, the driver, said quietly, "I can't get out, the gun's blocking the hatch," and I crawled back in to free him, and the four of us ran over terraces of black earth with the bullets flying around us, and Eli said, "I can't go on," and we forced him to. And how Syrian commandos jumped out of a helicopter right ahead of us. There was even more I wanted to tell him—of the thoughts I had, and the prayers I said, and the things I shouted to God and promised Him.

It was just that, each time, I thought: When I'm done the rabbi will ask in his gentle voice, "What happened to the friend who was with you that night?" And I would have to lower my eyes and tell him, "Dov is dead."

It would have made the old man sad. And so I never went to see him. I stuck to my *Talmud* with its laws of houses, cisterns, pits, and caves. The years went by. I couldn't put it off any longer. I'll go see him, I thought. Whatever will be, will be. I went to Bayit ve-Gan and found some Amshinov *Hasidim*.

"How is your rabbi?" I asked.

"Just a few hours ago," they told me, "his soul departed this world."

Chapter two

Be glad you're alive. *Wherefore doth a living man complain?* My shoulder gave a start. A hand touched it.

"Soldier, we're here. Soldier! Are you asleep?"

The driver shook my shoulder gently. "Can you hear me, soldier?"

"Yes. I hear you. I hear you."

"Gunner, do you hear me? Check the intercom in your helmet, gunner!"

"Yes, Gidi. I hear you. Roger."

I must have dozed off for a few seconds in the padded gunner's seat with my head on the armrest. There had been crazy days without sleep, one hand gripping the gun shield and the other the sights, the periscope battering my swollen eye each time the tank lurched over the black, terraced earth of Hushniya.

"Gunner, don't lose the horizon!" Gidi had shouted. "This is a war, not a maneuver. Do you hear me, gunner?"

7

"Yes, sir. I hear you. What should I aim at? Where?"

"I'm sorry, mister. I hear you. I must have been dreaming. Did you say we're in Bayit ve-Gan? So soon? Of course I know where it is. I grew up here."

I roused myself from sweet sleep in the soft, satiny seat of the new Volvo. I hadn't slept like that for ages. It was a hitchhiker's dream, a single ride from Tel Aviv's Geha Junction to Jerusalem's Bayit ve-Gan. I glanced at my watch. Eight P.M. I had sixteen hours of leave left. My first time home since *Yom Kippur*. So far, so good.

From Kfar Halis at the far end of the Syrian bulge to the town square in Kuneitra had taken an hour. I was driven by Hanan, my company commander. He was promoted after the war. The brigade second-in-command scrounged up three tanks for him. One was a cripple, its turret dangling to one side from the battle of Nafah quarry. The other two looked lame on their shortened treads too. Both had broken their sprocket drives on the old Tapline road. Hanan found the fourth tank himself. It had been sitting, unclaimed, in the repair shop with its gun swivel out of commission. That made three-tanks-and-a-half. In those days that passed for a company.

"Hanan!" the brigade commander had said in Kfar Halis. "Take any stray crew members you can find and put together a company. I'm giving you the command. You'll have to make do with what there is. I need a combat-ready force facing Tel Antar. We're not taking any more chances after this war. It's anybody's guess what happens next. I'm counting on you."

The news that Hanan was forming a company made the rounds of the battalion. He had been a platoon leader in the war. Now, he managed to cobble together a few crews of homeless tankers like myself. Any crew member can tell you what it's like to wander around a battalion with a tank helmet but no tank or crew. This was why, when we heard what Hanan was up to, we didn't ask the usual questions about who would be with us and in what sort of tank. All that mattered was to stop being errand boys for the staff sergeant and drifting from crew to crew as temporary replacements. To have our own tank again, with its name painted in black on white jute sacking tied to the rear ammunition hold, Hold Number 9. To switch on the radio and be able to say, "Roger, reading you loud and clear. Yes, 2-B, I read you. White Command will be there in two short ones. Over and out."

Our new company of refugees already had a name, just like in the good old days. We were back in the saddle, scarred and short a few tanks, but a company. Each morning before revving up the engines, we serviced them and tested our radios, like a real crew. Like once upon a time.

Hanan gathered us lovingly. He knew and felt what each of us had been through. He had advanced with us from Camp Yiftach on the night after *Yom Kippur* and had fought in the ambush at Nafah and the breakthrough at Khan Arnaba. The few drills he put us through didn't call for much comment on his part. We all knew our jobs. He never shouted at us. Whatever criticisms he had were conveyed gently. He wore fatigues and worked on the tanks with us, greasing, lubing, and changing sparkplugs. He stood watch with us too. Some mornings he came into our tents and shook us lightly to wake us.

Hanan and I didn't talk on the drive to Kuneitra. He was not a talkative type. In general, we didn't talk much after the war. He drove the jeep and I sat next to him. Once, taking a hairpin turn, he told me to look at how pretty the ravine below was. Oleanders were growing there in a thicket with other flowering shrubs.

We reached the square in Kuneitra. It was teeming with infantry. Men from the Golani Brigade were hitching rides. Hanan reached out to open my door, helped me to shoulder my pack, and slapped my back in a fatherly goodbye. "Have a good time," he said with a bashful smile. "Make sure you're back in twenty-four hours. Remember, the gunner of 2-A doesn't leave until you're here."

I didn't have to wait long in Kuneitra. An army transport pulled up and took us all. It was a good start. I hoped my luck would hold to Jerusalem. From Kuneitra to Rosh Pina took three-quarters of an hour. Rosh Pina wasn't far from Tiberias, and from Tiberias I could practically smell home.

I sat at one end of one of the two facing benches in the back of the truck with my pack on my knees, the rifle on my shoulder slapping against it while I listened to the men from the Golani Brigade talk. Each had a story to tell and they all interrupted each other. I liked being with them. They were loud and good-natured, simple and open with one another. I needed their kind of warmth to take my mind off my loneliness and sadness. I had never been so sad in my life.

The soldiers from the Golani Brigade reminded me of the teenagers who lived in the immigrant project of Beit Mazmil. After school they hung out on the chinning bars of the Tikvatenu Athletic Club, joking and laughing. The shortcut home from the *Talmud Torah* in Bayit ve-Gan passed by the club. I liked listening to them.

In those days I had just arrived in Israel from Egypt and didn't know up from down. I spent the days with Dov in the *Talmud Torah*, which took pride in its two luminaries, Rabbi Abramski and Rabbi Kunstrass; basked in the nearby *Hasidic* courts of Amshinov and Sokhetshov; and preened itself on the rich *Sephardic* families whose children attended its classes, the Einis and Aburabias and Havilios and Angels. Every evening I walked home past the project in Beit Mazmil, with its loud gangs swinging their legs from the chinning bars, Keslasi's gang and Dede's gang and Momo's gang.

On Friday nights I accompanied my father to his old Cairo Synagogue, Ahavah ve-Achvah. Wherever he went, his synagogue went with him, even to Beit Mazmil. And every Saturday I was back in Aleppo with my grandfather, listening to the sermons and songs and wondrous deeds and miracles of Hakham Attiya and Hakham Abudi.

I had many worlds within me in those days and I was happy in them all.

The soldiers from the Golani Brigade reminded me of the gangs from Beit Mazmil. They were just a bit older, with the first traces of sadness etched in their faces. I sat in the corner, minding my business. I wasn't infantry. A soldier called Momo told how, on the second day of the war, he was given an order by Staff Sergeant Na'imi, whose shoulder had been shot to pieces while taking a hilltop. "You remember? That's where Keslasi's men were put to cover us."

"The hell it was!" Several voices were shouting at once. "You're full of it! Keslasi was wounded that morning coming out of the wadi…"

"You bet it was Keslasi!" Momo stood his ground. "So he says to me, Na'imi, 'Momo,' he says, 'I'm being evacuated. You're in command.' 'What command?' I say. 'Command of who? I'm a private and there are five men left.' 'Then you're in command of all five,' Na'imi says. 'The CO was hit this morning, his second is with the covering force, and Ohayon's stuck below with three men who took a grenade.' He's telling me! 'Momo,' he says, 'don't let me down. You never have.' He's still talking when I hear Dede shout, 'Momo, on your right!' I belly flop onto a thorn bush and open up with the zero-three. You should have heard it go off!"

Momo, now the center of attention, was getting up a head of steam when a sleepy soldier in the back stirred and said:

"It was a miracle, Momo, that the zero-three didn't jam on you the way it did in Elyakim." He turned to the rest of the truck. "The leader of Third Platoon had to cross a barbed-wire fence in that exercise where the lead man lies on the wire and everyone leapfrogs over him. The major and the captain were up on a hill, looking through their binoculars at Platoon Three, which was supposed to lay down covering fire—and there's not a single shot. Remember how Na'imi kept us up in the rain until two in the morning cleaning our guns?"

Everyone laughed except me. I curled up even more in my corner until I was almost inside myself. I wasn't infantry. And if I was listening to Momo, it wasn't because I wanted to hear war stories. By now I knew that whoever fought in the war had no end of them, and whoever didn't, didn't believe them. Try telling someone that the third day of the war had found our crew, armed with a single grenade and two Uzis, one with a shoulder strap and one without, walking with a weird calm past the mud houses of Nafah back to our abandoned tank. There was a roar overhead. We looked up and saw a chopper land on the road in front of us. Before we knew it, dozens of Syrian commandos in battle gear were jumping out of it. We were wondering what to do when a Golani patrol, God only knows from where, turned up on a half-track with guns blazing. Try telling someone that we just kept walking to our tank as if nothing unusual had happened. Afterwards, we never even talked about it.

It took me a long time to be ready to tell or listen to war stories. Most people, I had noticed, thought the war so traumatized those of us who were in it that we made things up, or confused what we saw with what we thought we saw, and what we thought we saw with what we heard, until it all came out twisted and exaggerated.

I had no interest in infantry stories. But they did stir old memories. I recognized Momo's voice. His Moroccan accent brought back my childhood in Beit Mazmil. So did the ride from Rosh Pina to Tiberias, which was our first stop after arriving in Israel. I don't know why, but ever since the war all things remind me of my childhood. I kept staring at Momo. I was transported to a different world.

We were new in Beit Mazmil and in Jerusalem. Although the whole neighborhood consisted of new immigrants, we were the newest. Just the day before we had arrived from Tiberias. A woman named Bella, from the Jewish Agency in Haifa, had sent us there at night in a truck, straight from the Artza. No one else was in port to welcome us, neither Uncle Nino from Jerusalem, nor Uncle Zaki from Rehovot, nor Hakham Binyamin. They hadn't got our cable from Milan.

I remember it clearly. My mother stood by the truck with tears in her eyes. She had a crying infant in one arm and a sleeping baby on her shoulder. More children in woolen sweaters and caps from Milan were tugging at her dress while my father tried to comfort her with verses from the Bible about the wonders of the Land of Israel. Before that, he had spied a sailor in a spotless white uniform and gleaming insignia. Full of emotion, he had pointed to him proudly and explained to us, "Look, a soldier, an Israeli soldier!" He approached him and said, showing off the Hebrew that in Egypt he made a point of speaking on the Sabbath, "Soldier, how goes it?" The sailor regarded him with amazement and walked off. "May God prosper your ways, soldier!" my father called after him. "O valiant warrior!"

A few bumpy hours later we were in Tiberias. We climbed out of the truck and followed the porters, who carried, besides our big suitcases, six standard-issue beds, six straw mattresses, a kerosene cooking stove, and some utensils. They led us to a large shack, lit a kerosene lamp hanging on a wall, handed my father a pencil, had him sign a form, and disappeared.

We were left by ourselves. It was our first night in the Land of Israel. We were, my father said, in a fine place. The *Talmud* declared that Tiberias was a beautiful city and that Miriam's well bubbled up from the depths of its lake, the Sea of Galilee. Miriam's well was mentioned in the Bible—but did we know it was one of God's last creations as the sun set on the world's first Sabbath, after which it was magically transported to the desert of Sinai for the Children of Israel to have water when they wandered there? Not only was it the deepest well in the world, but the Redemption would commence from its depths. And since we now had our own Jewish state, the Redemption was under way. Moreover, in his digest of the laws of the *Talmudic* tractate of Sanhedrin, Maimonides mentioned a tradition that the Sanhedrin would be reconvened in Tiberias before moving to the rebuilt Temple in Jerusalem. And the Jewish Agency had told my father that he need find only ten pupils in Tiberias to be granted a teaching post. In Egypt he had been a mere businessman. This too was for the best.

My mother, however, announced that she was not staying another night in this place. I thought I saw a teardrop fall.

That night in Tiberias we had a visit from an old man. He had a white beard, kind eyes, and a long brown cloak with broad white stripes that looked like a cross between a caftan and a bathrobe. He lived, so he told us, by the lakeshore, near the old city wall, close to the synagogue of the Boyan *Hasidim*. Having heard that new immigrants had arrived from Egypt, he had come with a gift of fresh dates, some raisins, and a bottle of wine. Handing the dates to us children, he told us to hold them and recite, "Blessed art Thou O God, our Lord and King of the Universe, Who creates the fruit of the tree." He listened with his eyes shut while each of us said the blessing, uttered a fervent "Amen" at the end of it, and told us next to thank the Lord "Who has sustained us, and maintained us, and remained with us unto this day." The dates came from the vicinity of Tiberias, from the new harvest. We had been sustained and maintained not only long enough to eat them, but to obey the commandment to live in the Land of Israel, which it was our good fortune to be doing.

The old man urged my father to drink a glass of wine with him. A glass of wine, he said, was a great thing. It conjoined the hearts of men and this wine was the very best, made in Israel by the Carmel-Mizrachi Winery.

As there was no chair to offer the old man, and the beds were occupied by crying children, he and my father exchanged toasts standing up.

The old man shook my father's hand and drank to our lives. "Welcome to the Land of Israel!" he said.

"Well-being to the dwellers therein!" my father replied. "Here's to a good life, to peace, and to happiness!"

Expansively, my father told the old man that in Egypt, too, we had drunk Carmel-Mizrachi wine on Jewish feast days. Although on ordinary Sabbaths we had made do with homemade raisin wine, our holidays were marked with wine from Israel.

The dates now served for yet another blessing, this one for the *shivat haminim*, the seven agricultural products that the Land of Israel is renowned for. We did not end it, as is done in the lands of Exile, "For the land and the fruit of the vine," but rather, as is done in the Land of Israel, "For the land and the fruit of its vines."

The old man then asked for our names and inquired whether we knew the verses from the Bible that went with them. We did not. We had never heard that every name had a verse. Indeed it did, the old man said. Every Jew had his own verse from the Bible, the first and last letters of which were the same as those of his name. Whoever recited this verse three times a day at the end of the *Shmoneh Esreh,* the Eighteen Benedictions, would be sure to remember his name when he stood before the heavenly tribunal on Judgment Day. Your private verse stayed with you your whole life.

The old man took us one by one and gave each of us a verse. When it was my turn, I told him my name was Haim. He responded at once:

"Commit thy way unto the Lord, trust also in Him."

My father was delighted. "What did I tell you?" he said to my mother. "The people of the Land of Israel are fine folk. They know their Bible and the ways of hospitality. The land is a good one and Tiberias is a goodly city, on holy soil."

But my mother refused to be solaced. She didn't sleep a wink all night. Instead, she stayed up writing to her family. She couldn't understand what had happened to the cable from Milan.

The next day a taxi drove up to the shack. Everyone was in it, Nino, Zaki, and Hakham Binyamin. "Come!" they said. "We're taking you to Jerusalem. Now!" My father's protestations were useless. We were taken to Jerusalem. Our belongings followed us.

One thing led to another and we ended up in Beit Mazmil at the home of my uncle, Hakham Binyamin. Although the already crowded house now filled to overflowing, no one complained. We were children, and no sooner had we arrived than we went off with Shabtai, Hakham Binyamin's son, to the *Tikvatenu* Athletic Club. A loud group of boys was playing war on the soccer field and in the small park next to it. They had rifles made of fig branches and pine cone grenades, and one of them was the commander. We found a corner with a sandbox and sat talking quietly, as we were accustomed to doing in Egypt. Before we could relax, we were surrounded by some of the boys. They pointed at us and yelled:

"Arabs! Arabs!"

I burst into tears. I wanted to run but didn't know where. The commander said to us:

"Hey, take it easy! No one's going to hurt you, not Keslasi and not Dede. I'm Momo. From now on, you belong to our gang."

The boys regarded him admiringly. He explained:

"These kids aren't Arabs. They're talking Arabic because they're new. They haven't learned Hebrew yet."

"That's right," Shabtai agreed, hurrying to our defense. "They're my cousins from Egypt. They're staying with us. Leave them alone."

"Take it easy," Momo said again. "I'm commander. No one touches them."

The boys wandered off. I hadn't understood a thing. Who were they? Why did they have guns? Whom were they fighting? Who was Keslasi? And what did belonging to Momo's gang mean? Still in tears, I ran back to Hakham Binyamin's. My mother was in the yard, waiting for a vat of laundry water to come to the boil on a kerosene stove. In Egypt we had our own washerwoman.

"Mama!" I blurted. "They called us Arabs!"

The next time I saw Commander Momo was again at the *Tikvatenu* Athletic Club. He was playing soccer. The center forward on Tsachi's team, he advanced unopposed with the ball toward the other team's goal, the defense scattering before him. You could see that whoever tried getting in his way would be sorry.

In those days I was studying the Book of Joshua with my Uncle Jacques and the Book of Genesis, with the commentary of *Rashi*, with Rabbi Dikanoff in the *Talmud Torah*. A pupil—say Ben-Shoshan sitting next to me—would chant a verse from Genesis like *But the bird he divided not,* and Rabbi Dikanoff would read us *Rashi*'s interpretation: to wit, "Holy Writ is telling us that Israel is indestructible."

"And when the vultures came down upon the carcasses," I continued, taking up the chant, *"Abram drove them away."*

"What is Holy Writ telling us now?" Ben-Shoshan asked. And Keslasi added, "What's a vulture? And what's this *horror of great darkness* that fell on Abram?"

Rabbi Dikanoff ignored such questions. An ignored child asks again, and ignored a second time, he makes up his own answers. I was not only a child but an imaginative one, and as I pictured the

vultures swooping down on the carcasses, a horror of great darkness
fell on me. I tried fending it off unsuccessfully. Then it was recess
time.

During recess Madame Yisrael of the *Tikvatenu* Athletic
Club prepared thick slices of dark bread smeared with strawberry
jam, which she ladled out with a large spoon from a round tin can.
Each boy received a slice. Madame Yisrael had a good heart. She cut
the slices as thickly as she could and smeared them generously, but
even then there was always some left over. Everyone crowded around
for seconds. That was when Momo stepped in. The boys made way
and Madame Yisrael put him in charge. Pleading eyes vied for his
attention. No one had enough to eat at home.

My brothers and I stood off to one side. In Egypt we had been
taught not to push. And what chance did we stand anyway?

Momo noticed me. He was holding the last slice of bread and
jam. Without a word, he came over and gave it to me. That was when
I understood. We belonged to his gang. We were his.

Long afterwards, I was walking with Dov one day from Beit Mazmil
to the *Talmud Torah* in Bayit ve-Gan. We were discussing an article
Dov had read. This was years ago and I'm not sure I remember it.
It may have dealt with the question of whether human beings are
naturally good but corruptible, or naturally corrupt but improvable.
Something of the sort, anyway. Dov opened his bag, took out the
article, and showed it to me. We were reading it together, near Mount
Herzl, when we heard a sound. Someone was throwing stones. One
fell at our feet. It was the boys from the Ein Karem gang.

"Hey, professor! Shmofessor!" they yelled mockingly at Dov.
"You think your books will save you from the Ein Karem gang?"

They began walking toward us. We quickened our steps.

"You're chicken!" they called. "What will you do in the army?
Read books? Pray?"

"They'll be paratroopers," one boy said.

"Nah, tankers," said another.

They burst out laughing. "C'mon," someone yelled. "Let's take 'em prisoner."

They would have caught us if not for the miraculous appearance of Momo. At first this only frightened Dov more. "It's Momo," I assured him. "He's commander of the Beit Mazmil gang. We belong to him."

"Take it easy," Momo said. "I'll escort you." The boys from the Ein-Karem gang slunk away and we walked together in silence. Momo escorted us all the way to the *Talmud Torah*. We thanked him when we reached it and said goodbye. He turned to go, then turned back and murmured:

"Study well."

"Who was that?" Dov asked in amazement when he was gone. "Someone you know?"

I told Dov that Momo lived in the project building above Mr. Levi's vegetable store. He had been thrown out of the Yeshurun Elementary School for misconduct. The story was that he'd stubbed out a burning cigarette on a girl from 4-c. Now he roamed the neighborhood, flying kites and building skateboxes.

There was a steep road running from the project to the immigrant shantytown at the bottom of the hill. In winter the rains made a river of it. In summer the kids skateboxed down it. Once Momo invited me to join him on a new skatebox he had made out of boards from a vegetable crate given him by Mr. Levi. He had fitted it with wheels from an old baby carriage and made a rudder to steer with. I sat behind him, hugging his broad back. Somehow we kept from falling off. By the Sha'ar ha-Shamayim Synagogue, in which Hakham Binyamin was the rabbi, I asked to be let off.

"I have to say the afternoon prayer before sunset," I said.

Momo braked with a crunch of his feet in the gravel yard of the synagogue and said without looking back:

"Go, go pray. Don't think I can't pray too. My father's a cantor. He even writes hymns. Back in Morocco he had his own synagogue." As if to prove it, he sang in a sweet tremolo:

O when will word come
To the downtrodden dreamer
That salvation is nigh
And Zion has a redeemer,
That salvation is nigh
And Zion has a redeemer?

He followed it with another hymn:

Yea, every day I wait and pray,
My heart and soul so curious
To journey to that holy place,
The city of Tiberias.

He fell silent with a triumphant glance. I could tell he enjoyed my astonished look. He waited a while longer and then barreled on down to the shantytown.

Eight years went by. Our ways parted. Momo went to a vocational high school and Dov and I studied at the *yeshiva* in Bayit ve-Gan. I never ran into Momo again. And now here he was, holding forth in a truck full of soldiers between Kuneitra and Rosh Pina. He still had the same hearty laugh and the same way of singing his sentences as if each were a ballad in itself. I wasn't dreaming. It was him.

In the days after *Yom Kippur*, I had to warn myself not to dream. I had to keep my mind on the gun sights. My eye was tearing and the sights were blurred and my mind raced a mile a minute, but I knew I mustn't dream. The next Sagger missile could come from anywhere, like the one that hit Tank 3-A. But this was no dream. It was Momo, the commander of the Beit Mazmil gang.

"Remember that afternoon the major told us to turn around and make a beeline down the 'America' track to Nafah Junction because a chopper of Syrian commandos had touched down? We were there in two minutes. You should have seen us hit the ground in a row and let them have it point-blank from the road!"

I had to keep myself from jumping to my feet in the moving truck. A thought had occurred to me. No one in our battalion knew what had happened to Dov. His tank commander had been too badly wounded to talk. The rest of his crew had bailed out without seeing him. Miki, the brigade adjutant, also said he knew nothing, as did Kimmel, the battalion adjutant. I believed them. The confusion in Camp Yiftach in those first days of the war was unbelievable. Hysterical civilians wandered about, asking for sons and husbands. Tankers in stained, filthy suits sat holding their helmets beneath the eucalyptus trees, each in a world of his own. They had all lost their tanks and come down to Yiftach, and now they sat in eerie silence, red-eyed and caked with soot, waiting to take the tanks that came out of the repair shop back to the war. The civilians went among them, begging for scraps of information about the missing. I had seen Dov's brother there. Now, it occurred to me that maybe Momo knew something. I had heard that a Golani half-track had evacuated wounded tankers from Nafah Junction.

It was a long shot. Momo was infantry. Dov was armored corps. And yet anything was possible. Take Yossi's tank: leading the battalion that first night, it took a wrong turn at Wasit Junction, sped down the 'America' track to Kuneitra, ended up in the barnyard of Kibbutz Ein-Zivan between cows and Syrian tanks, and was retrieved by an infantry patrol that brought it back to Nafah.

But there was no chance to ask. Momo didn't stop talking. He told stories all the way to Rosh Pina. There we jumped from the truck by a gas station and he vanished in a crowd of soldiers. I searched for him, couldn't find him, and then spotted him running to catch a bus to Kiryat-Shmoneh. Before I could reach it, it had pulled away.

Too bad. Anything was possible. And what was Momo doing on a bus to Kiryat-Shmoneh? He was from Jerusalem, from Beit Mazmil.

I spent ten minutes at the PX in Rosh Pina. It was packed with soldiers and the lines were long. At last I reached the counter and ordered a cinnamon bun and coffee from an elderly woman volunteer who was doing her best to serve everyone at once. The coffee and bun tasted of freedom, even though I was a tea drinker who had never touched coffee before the war. In the army everyone drank it. Each morning the crew of Tank 3 made me join it for a cup of bitter black brew served in a demitasse set found by Zada at Khan Arnaba. No one understood how I could start the day without it.

In the PX I ran into Amichai, the loader of 1-B. He gave me a big hug. We drank our coffee staring at each other in silence. Neither of us mentioned the war. "Tell me the latest about property laws," Amichai finally said, our standard joke whenever we met in maneuvers. As if nothing had changed.

I hadn't seen him since the second day in Nafah. We were both in the force that was ambushed there. I had last caught sight of him being evacuated. He had managed to call out to me, *"Put your trust in the Lord!"* I wanted to finish the verse and call back, *"Be strong, and take heart, and trust,"* but shells were flying all around us and Gidi shoved my head back into the tank.

"Amichai took shrapnel in the leg," our loader Eli told me enviously over the intercom. "He's out of the war."

When Amichai reached Kibbutz Gadot in the Hula Valley and told the kibbutzniks that our tanks were in flames at Nafah and the Syrian army had reached the old Customs House near the Jordan, they shook pitying heads. Everyone thought he was shell-shocked. Who could believe him? Two days later he escaped from the hospital, hitchhiked back up to the battlefield, found a tank in need of a driver, and fought for the rest of the war, right through the breakthrough at Khan Arnaba. He came bearing gifts. With him were the *Arbat Haminim*, the Four Species, the palm shoot, citron, myrtle, and willow branch, needed for the Feast of *Sukkot*. Nearly the whole battalion said the blessing over them in a tabernacle we built in Alika from tent flaps and branches spread over a hole made by a mortar shell. Alika was our jumping-off point for the final push. Perhaps the Sages had that in mind when they said, "Like a warrior seizing his weapon, so do the People of Israel seize the palm shoot after *Yom Kippur*."

A half-hour passed in Rosh Pina waiting for a ride. Long lines of soldiers stood in a driving rain. My windbreaker and uniform were soaked through. But who cared? I was going home. My mother would throw everything in the wash. A cold wind blew in my face. Let it blow. If I had lived through the war, I wasn't going to die from catching cold now.

It took two hours to reach Ra'anana Junction in an army Renault. No one talked. Everyone looked depressed. At the junction I went off and said an early afternoon prayer, as is permitted when there may not be time later. We soldiers had become used to that. We prayed when we could. You never knew when you would have another chance.

I tried to focus on my prayers. It was hopeless. As soon as I shut my eyes, I began seeing things. Dov was in every scene. My thoughts went from Camp Yiftach to Nafah and from Nafah to our tank. I couldn't concentrate. And the war had taught me what concentration in prayer was: in the ambush in Nafah quarry, with no radio, with an auxiliary charger for ignition and unadjusted gun sights and the missiles coming closer and the tanks around us bursting into flames. Gidi had shouted:

"Gunner, pray! We're taking fire!"

I prayed. There wasn't a hair's breadth then between my heart and my lips. I had never prayed like that before.

It took a while to get out of Ra'anana Junction. Cars passed without stopping. Didn't anyone see me? I was from the war! I was going home! Please, stop, I have only twenty-four hours. Perhaps there would be time to drop by my *yeshiva*. The headmaster might be there. I had so much to tell him—about what we had been through, and how I now viewed my studies, and the difference between book faith and heart faith.

Toward the end of the *Yom Kippur* service, our headmaster had said to us:

"We studied in the tractate of *Yoma* how Rabbi Akiva says: 'Fortunate are you, O Israel! Before Whom do you purify yourself and by Whom are you purified? Your Father in Heaven, for it is written: *And I shall sprinkle on you purifying waters and purify you.*' And we read too: *For Israel's ablution is the Lord.* Just as the waters of ablution

purify the unclean, so the Holy One Blessed Be He purifies Israel."
Our headmaster cited a *Hasidic* rabbi who once said, "As a person
enters the ritual bath with no clothes between him and the water, so
nothing comes between Israel and its Father in Heaven when it is
purified." It was thus that the Sages explained the verse in the Song
of Songs, *Open to me, my sister, my bride.* They said: "God tells Israel,
Make an opening for me as small as the eye of a needle and I will
make one for you large enough for a wagon to pass through." To
which the same *Hasidic* rabbi added: "Although the eye of a needle
is small, it has no impediments."

The headmaster's sermon spoke to me. I thought I understood
what a heart with no impediments was. Now I knew I had understood
nothing. And I thought: I'll tell the headmaster what I know now.

Sometimes, in the worst moments, it had helped me to write
poetry. I didn't show it to anyone. I'll show it to my headmaster, I
had thought. He'll read what I can't tell him face to face.

I would show him what I wrote about my friend Shaya, whose
death I had heard about from Roni on the first day of the Feast of
Sukkot. When I think of Shaya I think of the verse in Lamentations,
*The precious sons of Zion, comparable to fine gold, how they are now like
earthen pitchers, the work of the hands of the potter.* For two years we
had studied together, day and night, in the *yeshiva.* The news of his
death made me shut my eyes tight and bury my head in my hands.
I saw him before me, a golden youth, with a tall palm shoot in one
hand and a fine citron in the other. The air was perfumed with myrtles.
The green branches of our tabernacle formed a protective roof over
us. Suddenly a gale blew, throwing the world into confusion. The
heavens opened and torrents of rain ran down our faces. The tent
pegs flew loose and the flaps collapsed, scattering the branches. Bitter laughter rumbled from the four ends of the sky. "Where is your
tabernacle now?" it said. I sat down and wrote:

With prayer-shawl gowns
And palm shoot in hand,
Their shelter has flown.

All the walls have come down.
For protection they stand
Beneath heaven's dome.

I glanced at my watch. The hands were moving. My twenty-four hours were ticking away and I was stuck at Ra'anana Junction. "Look, men," Hanan had said to us the night before when, afraid to be disappointed, no one had wanted to draw the first slip of paper from his fatigue cap. "The major says twenty-four hours. That's it. We're holding the line here by ourselves. There's no one to relieve us. Our whole battalion is down to little more than a company. I've heard they're shortening tankers' courses and converting mechanized brigades to tank crews. Maybe in a few weeks we'll get new crewmen with some experience and be able to take longer leaves. Right now, that's all we have. Twenty-four hours. It's a shame to waste a minute of it, so let's get on with the draw. Who's first?"

Now my leave was slipping away at Ra'anana Junction. Finally, a Jew from Canada pulled up in a rented Ford Escort. He had been in Israel two days and was traveling up and down, looking for soldiers in need of lifts. He couldn't stay in Canada at such a time. "Tell me about the army," he said. "Were you in the war?"

Please, I thought. Leave me alone. I'm tired. It's too much for me. What was I going to tell him? How?

"Tell," he repeated.

I'll tell him just one thing, I thought. I began and I didn't stop. He drove in silence while I talked on and on. About climbing to the Heights from Yiftach in the hours before dawn on the night after *Yom Kippur*, the tanks traveling on their treads as though they were on parade instead of on a flatbed, the stars overhead and elderly kibbutzniks from Machanayim tossing us green apples and wishing us luck with their eyes. Roni, our driver, had a small volume of Maimonides. He read aloud from it the passage with which our headmaster had parted from us after the *Havdalah* blessings ending *Yom Kippur*. Our headmaster had gathered us in the library of the *yeshiva* and said:

24

"My sons, there is much that I could say to you. And yet our Sages tell us, 'In parting, always end with words of *Torah*, for in that way you will be remembered.'"

He opened a volume of Maimonides and read:

"'He who embarks on the path of war, let him put his trust in the Hope of Israel who will rescue him from all harm. And let him know that he is fighting for the unity of God's name. And let him risk what he must with no fear or thought for his wife and children...And may he clear his mind of all thoughts but those of war.... For he must know that the blood of Israel is upon his shoulders....'."

As we crossed the bridge over the Jordan, we saw combat engineers preparing it for demolition. Eli interrupted Roni to ask me if I saw what he did. "Yes," I said. We threw questioning looks at Gidi. He had seen it too. "Loader, tighten the machine gun," he told Eli. "It's loose. Take a wrench from the tool compartment and fix it." Roni kept reading from Maimonides. "'For should he not be victorious because he failed to go to war with all his heart and soul, he has as though spilled the blood of Israel, for it is written, *Let him not melt his brother's heart as his own.*'"

Past the bridge, we saw a tank coming toward us. We had never seen anything like it. Dazed soldiers with bruises and bandages sat or stood on the turret, the sprocket wings, and the ammunition hold and flagged us down. "Where are you going?" they yelled. "Are you out of your minds? There are Syrian tanks up ahead at the Customs House. We were caught in a pincer movement. They've taken Nafah. They'll head for Tiberias. Turn back, quick!"

We didn't know what to say. Spooked, we looked at Gidi. He said quietly, as if he had heard and seen nothing:

"Keep going, driver. Straight ahead."

I told all this to the Canadian Jew between Ra'anana and Geha Junction. There I said, "Thank you. I get off here. I'm going to Jerusalem."

The Jew's eyes had tears in them.

"Soldier!" he said in broken Hebrew. "Soldier! I also to do."

He looked at me pleadingly, as if waiting to be told what to do. When I made no response, he reached into his pocket, pulled out a wad of green dollar bills, and stuck them in my hand. "Take, soldier!" he said.

I pulled my hand away. "What's the matter with you, mister?" I nearly shouted. "Do you think I'm a charity case?"

He was crying now. "Soldier, please! Take! I must. Give to your friends. For cigarettes. For chocolate. I also to do. Please. Take!"

He hugged and kissed me. His tears were salty on my lips.

At Geha Junction I was given the lift in the Volvo. Now I was in the homestretch. I leaned back and let my eyes shut, gripping my rifle. Then someone was waking me. Where was I?

"Didn't you hear me, soldier?" the driver of the Volvo scolded. "We're here. No time for dreaming. This is where you get off. Do you know where you are? We're on Hapisgah Street in Bayit ve-Gan, near the Amshinov Synagogue. It's almost time for the evening prayer."

He glanced at me and added lamely: "I mean, if you want to pray. If you can."

"I'm sorry," I said. "I must have been dreaming. Of course I know where I am. Dov and I went to *Talmud Torah* here. It was from here that we left for the war."

He looked at me. "For the war? From the *Talmud Torah*? Left for where?"

It was my turn to be startled. "What do you mean, for where? For the Golan. For the war. Dov and I. We were assembled here, outside the synagogue. We sanctified the new moon of *Tishrei*."

"The new moon of *Tishrei*?" said the driver of the Volvo. "It's now the new moon of *Heshvan*. You haven't been home for a month?"

Had a whole month gone by? Anything was possible. It must have gone by if he said it had. He had been in Jerusalem and had seen it pass. He said:

"Listen, soldier. The Amshinov *Hasidim* will be praying in another minute. You can sanctify the new moon with them. In winter it isn't worth waiting. Seize the commandment when you can. You never know in rainy weather."

I glanced at my watch. "That's true," I said. "You never know."

I had sixteen hours left. Soon I'd be home. Everyone would be waiting for me. They were expecting me. I'd phoned from the PX in Rosh Pina. My grandfather would be there too, reciting Psalms. My mother said he hadn't stopped since *Yom Kippur.* He wouldn't stop until I came home, she said. But I had better sanctify the moon first. You never knew.

Chapter three

The evening prayer was over. The Amshinov *Hasidim* repaired to the synagogue courtyard. They sanctified the new moon of *Heshvan*, dancing with their hands on one another's shoulders. They lifted their heels off the ground and sang:

> *Goodly are the lights created by our Lord.*
> *With foresight did He make them, with wisdom and with skill.*
> *Strength did He give them and vigor to prevail,*
> *Ruling in Heaven according to His will.*
>
> *Brimming with glory and with radiance,*
> *Forth go their beams until the Heaven's ends.*
> *Gladly they rise and gladly do they set,*
> *Dutifully performing their Master's errands.*
>
> *A good and blessed new month!*
> *A good and blessed new month!*

I danced with them. On one shoulder danced my pack and on the other my rifle. I didn't want to seem aloof, even though I knew that they and I no longer shared the same world. I was coming home from *Yom Kippur.*

The *Hasidim* blessed each other in parting. I blessed them and was blessed too, feeling that every blessing was meant just for me. For me God had made the sun and the moon. For me they rose and they set. I was coming home from the war.

The *Hasidim* drifted off. I was left by myself. Even though I had a home to go to, I remained standing there. The willow branches and pine cones on the ground gave off a keen smell. The moon shone down. I breathed deeply, as if to feel or stop the flow of time. What I thought I could stop from flowing, I didn't know.

It was from this place, a month ago, that we had set out. The moon of *Tishrei* had shone on Dov and me. Now it was the moon of *Heshvan* and it was engulfed by clouds. I shouldered my pack and rifle. If I took the Number 18 bus from Mount Herzl to Beit Mazmil, I was sure to run into someone I knew. I wanted to walk down the hill from Bayit ve-Gan. I needed to spend these last minutes with myself. Anyone I ran into on the bus would want to know where I had been, and where I was going, and what I had been doing, and what did I think. What would I say? That I had been in the war? That I had met my own self there?

Perhaps I would tell them about fear. Or death. And crying out to God and missing Dov. In the middle of a packed bus, with a pop tune playing on the radio and the driver shouting "Move to the rear" to some woman with shopping bags who wouldn't budge from the door because she wasn't sure she could fight her way back to it. It was better to walk. I needed to put my thoughts in order.

The cool night air of Bayit ve-Gan felt good to me. It was part of my childhood. So were the rocks that gleamed at me in the darkness. They were old friends. On sunny winter days Dov and I used to return from the *Talmud Torah* this way, skipping from rock to rock. We preferred it to the stuffy, crowded buses with their tired, irritable passengers. We liked treading on the bare rocks with the pretty cyclamens peeping from beneath them. The air smelled of wildflowers. After the cyclamens came the bright red poppies. The sun was good and warm and we liked being together.

I loved listening to Dov talk. He read everything he could get his hands on, science and philosophy and astronomy and geology and *Hasidic* tales and the latest *Torah* commentaries, and he discussed them all with the same shy, dreamy look. It was always new and stimulating for me. We didn't study or talk about such things in the *Talmud Torah* or at the Tikvatenu Athletic Club. You could only learn them from the magazines Dov read. In return I told him stories from Egypt and Aleppo, mixed with my grandfather's sermons. On Brazil Street, Dov said, you didn't hear such things either.

Once, when we were stationed at Ras Sudar, the two of us were assigned to a checkpoint in the middle of the desert. We spent a week there, doing six-hour shifts. Everyone felt sorry for us. Nothing, not even Kitchen Patrol, was hated more. The soldiers we relieved warned us against letting the quiet drive us crazy. Not a living soul passed that way. No one knew what the checkpoint was for. Most likely there had once been a road and an order to guard it that had never been rescinded. "Take a lot to read," we were told.

We had a wonderful week. We took the tractate of *Ketubot* with the commentaries of Alfasi, Asher ben Yehiel, and Nissim of Gerona, along with The *Maharal* of Prague's *Eternity of Israel*. Dov also brought all kinds of reprints and bound and unbound sets of new and old journals full of interesting things. We talked all week. We were young, we were friends, and we were innocent, and we sat in the sand discussing faith, and knowledge, and life, and science, and the People of Israel, and Redemption, and the tractate of *Ketubot*, and our own lives, and what we would do with them, and how we had talked about the same things as two boys skipping over the rocks from Bayit ve-Gan to Beit Mazmil.

I skipped over them now too. There was just no one else with me. My rifle bumped against my pack with every step. I glanced at the sky. Dark clouds were trying to swallow the moon. Sometimes it got away and sometimes it didn't, so that it vanished and came back. Each time it shone again the world grew bright and I felt alive and free. Then it disappeared and there was darkness. The horrors of the war returned, as they did every night in my dreams.

I saw Tiktin, his body in flames, rolling on the ground with a jerry can of water. And there was Gidi shouting, "Fire, gunner! Fire! We're being shot at," and myself shouting back, "I don't know what to aim at," and the turret of the tank next to us flying in the air and landing in a fireball, and Roni saying, "I can't get out, the gun's blocking the hatch." And Dov's mother filling a box with cheese pastries, and his father kissing him, and Dov waving goodbye at Camp Yiftach, and the battalion second telling him to hurry and join his crew while he lingered a moment longer to say to me, "I wish we could have been together." I wished it too. And there was the glare of the rising sun in the gun sights, and me straining every muscle to see, but there was nothing but glare, and somewhere the gunner of a T-54 was placing his crosshairs on us. I had to find him. It was up to me. Another second and he would fire. I couldn't see a thing. Verses and snatches of Psalms came to my lips. *He will not suffer thy foot to stumble. He that keeps thee will not slumber. The Lord is thy shade upon thy right hand. I wait for the Lord, my soul does wait, and in His word do I hope. He shall cover thee with His pinions and under His wings thou shall trust. His truth shall be thy shield and buckler. The angel of the Lord encamps round them that fear Him and delivers them. The angel of the Lord encamps round them that fear Him and delivers them. The angel of the Lord...* My ears were aching from a helmet a size too small that I had grabbed from a supply bin in Yiftach while the battalion second shouted, "Move it! Take any equipment and move!" He alone knew what was happening at Nafah. Who had time to try on helmets?

The earphones pressed against my ears. A loud babble came through them in Arabic, Russian, and Hebrew. There were orders and shouts and static and explosions and even once—God knows from where—quiet music. I strained to make out Gidi's voice in the confusion. I didn't know what to aim at.

"I see him!" I cried. "I see him!"

The silhouette appeared in the lense for no more than a fraction of a second. It was enough. "Gunner firing!" I pressed the trigger. "High, down a half, fire!" "Down a half, firing!" "Direct hit! Direct hit! Cease your fire!" And then a loud boom. And Gidi shouting, "We've been hit! Abandon tank!"

Chapter four

I shook off my thoughts and yielded to the feeling of freedom. I was going home. The closer I came to Beit Mazmil, the lighter my feet grew. They were carrying me on their own. By the time I reached the paved path by the Tikvatenu Athletic Club, I was flying along the Jerusalem flagstone as though it recognized my steps. The oleander bushes waved. The cypress tree nodded as I passed.

It had been a *Bar Mitzvah* present from Mr. Babani. Everyone else had brought me books and Babani came with a cypress tree. I planted it that same day with Mr. Revach, the liturgy and gardening teacher at the Yeshurun Elementary School. Every month I measured my height against it.

Whoever I passed on the path said, "Shalom."

"Shalom, shalom," said my two guardian angels, the pair given me according to the verse, *For He shall give His angels charge over thee, to keep thee in all thy ways.* I parted with them at the front door. *Rest here in peace, angels of peace, angels of the Most High. Blessed be He who requites the unworthy with His goodness, for He has requited me only with good.* I knocked and entered. I had pictured this moment so many times that it almost seemed that it had already taken place. My mother, too excited to show her emotion, greeted me as matter-of-factly as if I had come home from the *Talmud Torah* in Bayit ve-Gan. I knew what a river of tears was hiding behind her calm, waiting to overflow. I went to kiss my father's hands. How proud he had been on the day I became a soldier and on the day I came home on my first leave in a uniform with the initials of the Israel Defense Force. Who thought about wars then? Now he was tense and restrained. He, too, needed all the strength he could muster to retain the composure that was betrayed only by his lips murmuring Psalms. I could practically guess which ones they were.

I stood in the living room looking at the round table that I had bought my parents with the money earned from a dull summer job sorting mail in the post office. It was still covered with the white tablecloth, embroidered with lovely pink and blue flowers, that my mother never took off. She had made it right after her wedding and had insisted on cramming it into the only suitcase she was allowed to take when leaving Egypt. The suitcase, which she had three hours to pack before boarding a freighter, the *Sudan,* bound for Greece and Italy, was bursting already. Only aboard ship would she be reunited with my father, who was being deported straight from prison. He had been accused of Zionist activities, although his only crime was being the sexton of the Ahavah ve-Achvah Synagogue and loving the Land of Israel.

I glanced at the wooden bowl of fancy fruit that my father replenished each day, whether or not it was empty, from the Mahaneh Yehuda market. The abundance of fruit in the Land of Israel, he never tired of telling us, was a sure sign of the Redemption, for it said in the tractate of *Sanhedrin*: "Rabbi Abba says, the coming of the Messiah will be evident to all, for it is written, *And ye, O mountains of Israel, ye shall shoot forth your branches and yield your fruit to my people of Israel, for they are at hand to come.*"

I looked longingly at my set of the *Talmud*, which stood on the shelf in its reddish-brown covers that I had lovingly fitted with plastic dust jackets, tractate by tractate. Seeing them gave me a warm feeling. I was home.

And yet…what was happening? Why did I also see gray mud huts on stony black earth, and ammunition holds with camouflage nets, and metal boxes of machine gun bullets being handed by me, two at a time, to Eli stacking them in the tank? Why did my fingers feel the cool, slick dew gleaming on the metal mount of the bazooka? From where did I get a heady whiff of the Turkish coffee with cardamon being boiled by Tzion on the tank engine as it warmed, mingled with the sweet smell of machine gun oil and the grease smeared on my overalls? And what made me taste the sour bitterness of grapefruit sections taken from a can pried open with a gunner's screwdriver and passed back and forth among the four of us?

I refocused on my mother, who kept running her eyes over me to make sure I was really there. She hovered about me, looking for words. Although she wanted so badly to find them, the only ones she could think of in the end were:

"So! Home again, eh? How are you?"

And I, too, could only answer: "Yes. I'm home. Thank God, I'm fine."

There were a few more moments of stiff silence and then the three of us erupted in a torrent of words. They tumbled out so fast that that part of the mind that weighs the need to speak against its hazards could not keep up with them. I don't know what I said. I only know that whatever it was, it still couldn't make my mother believe I had been in a war. At most she was ready to concede that I was somewhere in the rear, in a last line of defense reached by no one.

I was still slipping off my pack when the door swung open and in burst my headmaster with a group of students. I had no idea how they had got wind that I was there. Someone also went to bring my grandfather, who lived nearby. He came and sat without a word, probing me with dark, worried eyes. They were not severe and exacting as they usually were, but soft and clement as I remembered them from the *Yom Kippur* service when he threw himself on God's mercy.

37

Overcome with emotion, I wanted to run and hug everyone. I felt a new bond with them all, a love I never had felt before.

The room kept getting noisier. Everyone had things to ask me and to tell me. Everyone answered everyone else's questions, leading to arguments. Flying high in a world of my own, I talked on without hearing. The room buzzed with verses from the Bible, and with sayings of the Sages, and with stories of friends from my *yeshiva* who were stationed on the Canal when the war broke out. As though through a fog I saw my mother, her eyes pleading with me to drink my tea and eat the sesame rings she had baked especially for me, and my father sitting tearfully off to the side.

The headmaster raised a hand. There was a hush. He said:

"When our master King David, as a young shepherd tending his father's flock, rescued a lamb from the paws of a lion and a bear, he made of it a sheepskin coat and wore it to remind himself of the mercies of God. It was this coat that he had in mind when he said in his Psalms, *I shall not die but live and declare the works of the Lord.*"

The headmaster pointed at me and said:

"Declare the works of the Lord!"

An eager circle formed around me. I suppose they thought they were going to hear war stories.

"All right," I said. "I'll start with the first night of the war. We drove our tanks to Nafah. The darkness was lit by explosions. Tanks were burning everywhere. Wounded soldiers on the ground called out to us not to run over them with our treads. They were waiting to be evacuated. Someone flagged us down and we stopped. A powerfully built man with a large head and a gentle voice climbed onto the turret. He asked us to form a group around him. We were exhausted, and above all, in shock. We hadn't imagined war would be like this. The man shook each of our hands and said, 'Hello. I'm the colonel. I'm in command of your brigade.' We stared at him. No colonel had ever talked to us like that before."

Our last brigade commander before the war was a colonel too. We met him in May, shortly before Independence Day. Our brigade was holding the Canal. Dov and I were in a company assigned to a fortified bunker. Being an inexperienced unit, we were reinforced by a detachment of reserve paratroopers. The army was in a state of alert. There were reports of enemy troop movements. We were told the colonel was coming to inspect us.

We spent a whole day scrubbing the bunker. We polished the kitchen, re-stacked the ammunition, and cleaned our rifles. An hour before the colonel was supposed to arrive, we were assembled outside the bunker. For two hours we waited in the burning sun. At last he came. Without introduction he declared in a gruff voice, "The Egyptians are attacking from there." He pointed at the Canal. "What do you do?"

Soldiers tried answering. They would run to this or that position and open fire with this or that machine gun. The colonel cut them short. "You're surrounded by dozens of Egyptian tanks," he said scornfully. "Egyptian infantry is pouring in from there." He pointed to the front gate. "Hundreds of soldiers are crossing the Canal right in front of you." He gestured in its direction. "What good is a machine gun? Well, what do you do? Sit on your butts?"

No one knew. One man had the courage to ask:

"What, really, do we do?"

There were guffaws from some of the officers. One said:

"Relax! You'll leave it to your betters to do the job."

The visitors from the brigade left. Life went back to normal: guard duty, kitchen duty, roll call, and in between, chatting outside while eating green apples from a vat of chlorinated water. Everyone forgot the colonel. Almost everyone, anyway.

That night I had the last watch in the west sentry post facing the Canal. It was a watch I liked. You got to see the dawn break slowly in the darkness and the first glimmers of the sun.

Everything was routine. The silence was complete except for the occasional splash of a fish. Before dawn I took out my prayer shawl and *tefillin* and waited for there to be enough light for the morning prayer, which was defined by the rabbis as sufficient to make out a familiar face at a distance of four ells. Not that the soldier who now approached me was exactly familiar. He was tall and stoop-shouldered with large, intelligent eyes, and I recognized him as a second lieutenant in the paratroopers. We stood there talking. He was, he said, an undergraduate philosophy major. He had heard I was a *yeshiva* student and had studied Maimonides. There were some things he wanted to discuss with me.

We talked about Maimonides' view of individual Providence. If Maimonides really believed, the second lieutenant said, that the world was governed by the laws of nature, how could God suspend them for a specific individual? Nature's laws applied equally to everyone.

I gave him the answer I had been taught. There were, I said, different approaches to the problem. Maimonides' was that God's Providence sometimes extended to individual cases, but only with human beings. He himself, Maimonides wrote in his *Guide To The Perplexed*, was surprised by his own conclusions regarding the relationship between the intellectual knowledge of God and the divine emanation bestowed on the knower.

We debated that for a while. The second lieutenant pointed out inconsistencies in my position and I tried to harmonize them. One of his objections stumped me. I was mulling it over when he said out of the blue:

"The Egyptian attack will begin at exactly this hour of dawn. It will come from over there." He turned to look at our bunker, gazed out at the Canal, and continued as though to himself: "Everyone is asleep. It's perfectly calm. But I'm not. I've read the intelligence reports. I don't like it. These past few nights I've been up before dawn, making the rounds and watching the Canal. Did you hear what the colonel said today? He said that if dozens of Egyptian tanks were to cross at this point, there would be nothing we could do about it. Everyone laughed. But I didn't think it was funny. I can see those tanks crossing now, on pontoon bridges, right in front of us. I can see the attack being launched. Don't ask me how we'll stop it. I wish this stint of reserve duty was over. The others call me 'the Philosopher.'

Maybe they're right to make fun of me. Still, I don't know who they think is going to save them."

Without waiting for an answer, he repeated:

"I don't like it one bit."

And he was gone.

The midnight encounter at Nafah was different. The powerful man climbed onto the tank, his face covered with grime, and said: "Hello, I'm the colonel."

He took out a bar of chocolate and gave each of us a piece. "I know this must be hard for you," he said. "It's hard for me and you're still young. I've been in some tough battles, but I've never seen any like this. Our brigade has lost a lot of tanks. There's no chain of command any more. Your battalion and your company have lost their COs. It's hard, all right. But I'm certain we'll win. The winner will be whoever holds out the longest. Whoever doesn't break first. And that will be us. It has to be. We have no choice. The people of Israel depend on you. We're going to regroup with the tanks we have left and attack toward the Hushniya pocket before dawn. One company will move along the road and the other will cover it from the ridgeline. That's you. You can count on the Syrians firing missiles at you. I know you didn't train for that. No one warned you about it. But there's no need to panic. There's a way of dealing with it. Listen carefully. When the enemy fires a Sagger, he guides it by a wire held like this." The colonel demonstrated with two fingers. "If you fire back at him" (he elevated the machine gun on the turret and aimed it at an imaginary point), "he'll lose his concentration and miss. I did it yesterday with two missiles launched from the embankment along the Tapline road and it worked. You just have to maintain steady fire." Quietly he took each member of the crew aside and explained it to him again. Then he said:

"I'll say goodbye now. I love you all. We'll head out before sunrise. Don't forget to service your tanks. I'll have the infantry refuel them. You have four hours to sleep. Make good use of them. Tomorrow will be a long day. Get some shuteye. And don't leave your tank. That's an order. I want an armed crewman on the turret at all times. There are reports of helicopter-borne Syrian commandos in the area. Any questions?"

There were plenty of them, but no one asked. This wasn't the time for it. The colonel shook our hands and said again:

"Goodbye, men. I love you all."

He jumped lightly down from our tank and clambered onto another. We serviced the engine, sat on the turret, opened a tin of dry wafers, said the blessing over bread, and ate. It was our first meal since ending the fast. Roni gave a quick *Torah* lesson to keep us from being like the thoughtless souls referred to by the Sages when they said, *Whoever breaks bread without discussing Torah might as well partake of heathen sacrifices*. He posed a *Talmudic* problem and gave the answer. Then Gidi said:

"We're all dead on our feet. We have four hours. That's three to sleep in and one to stand watch. I'll take the first shift, so that I can get three straight hours. I'll need them tomorrow. You can divide the other watches any way you want."

That was fair enough. We went off to get what troubled sleep we could without taking off our boots or tankers' suits. Roni slept in the driver's compartment, Eli lay on a sprocket wing, and I curled up in the gunner's compartment with one shoulder against the gun shield and my head on the sights. We had done that in maneuvers. That was how you slept in a war, we were told. Gidi took the first watch.

At four A.M. we awoke to the sound of tank engines. "Start her up!" Gidi prodded us. "Prepare the shells. Fill the jerry can. We're moving out."

We stared at each other uncomprehendingly. "Gidi!" someone said. "What happened? Why didn't you wake us?"

It dawned on each of us at the same moment that he had stood watch all night. Shyly he said:

"You looked so tired and you're so young. You're babies, all of you. How was I going to wake you?"

I was finished. I looked around. No one spoke. The students from the yeshiva were puzzled. It wasn't what they had expected. Where were the heroics and the fireworks? But Grandfather nodded.

The headmaster noticed him and said:

"Haim's grandfather will say some words of wisdom."

At first Grandfather said nothing. His dark eyes probed the room. A moment passed before we heard his deep voice. It was not saying words of wisdom. It was improvising on the *Hallel* prayer—not to the usual holiday chant but to Grandfather's special melody for "In Fear A Crown They Give Thee" as it was sung in the *Yom Kippur* service in the Sha'ar ha-Shamayim Synagogue of Beit Mazmil. It was a melody that had sent shivers down my spine as a child. Grandfather sang:

> *I have called upon the Lord in distress; the Lord answered me and set me in a large place.*
> *The Lord is on my side; I will not fear; what can man do unto me?*
>
> *All the nations compassed me, but in the name of the Lord will I destroy them*—in the War of Independence.
>
> *They compassed me about, yea, they compassed me about, but in the name of the Lord will I destroy them*—in the Sinai Campaign.
>
> *They compassed me about like bees; they are quenched as the fire of thorns; for in the name of the Lord will I destroy them*—in the Six Day War.
>
> *Thou hast thrust sore at me that I might fall; but the Lord helped me*—in this war of *Yom Kippur.*
>
> *The Lord is my strength and song, and is become my salvation*—in time to come.

Grandfather was finished. I felt as though the rest of the Hallel prayer were coming to me and pleading "Me too!" and I picked up where he left off: *"The Lord has chastened me sore, but He has not given me over unto death."* Then the image of Dov appeared before me. He was standing beside the verse with his big, brown, dreamy eyes, *The Eternity of Israel* opened before him as at the checkpoint near Ras Sudar.

I fell silent. The room emptied out. The house grew still. My mother beckoned me to another room. She looked at me in a way she had never done before and said:

"What happened to Dov?"

"I don't know," I told her. "No one does. I wasn't with him."

"You were always together," she insisted. "You have to tell me what happened to him."

I realized that Dov's mother must have been calling her every day. She looked at me hard, searching my eyes for an answer, convinced by my evasiveness that I was concealing something.

There was no way to explain to her that I really didn't know. Who could explain what had happened that day?

"You have to talk to her," my mother said.

"What will I tell her when I don't know anything?"

I knew what would happen. I would go to her and she would say:

"You were always in the same tank. You left for the war together. You came back without him. Where is he?"

Chapter five

The opening blessings of the Morning Prayer are different from any others. Their language is special and so is their aim. A man says them after rising from sleep, when his soul is pure and his heart is aimed at his Creator and nothing has had time to sully the world or come between him and God. At such moments he remembers the sweetness of praying as a child, pure, innocent, and unburdened by sin.

Most special of all are the two prayers, "I give thanks before Thee" and "My Lord, the soul that Thou hast given me." There is nothing else like them: *I give thanks before Thee, O living and eternal King, for You have returned my soul within me with compassion—abundant is Your faithfulness!* This prayer was composed by the rabbis of Safed, who had in mind the verse from the Bible, *They are new every morning; abundant is Your faithfulness.* Every morning a man rises with a new soul and a new faith. The faith of today is not the faith of yesterday. Each day a man sees and hears and thinks many new things. New things happen and his faith is new too.

I once heard of a *Hasidic* rabbi who took hours to recite this prayer, for as soon as he began with the words "I give thanks before Thee" he thought: "Who is I? And who is Thee?"

Then comes, "My Lord, the soul that Thou did give me is pure. Thou did create it, Thou did form it, Thou did breathe it into me, and Thou does sustain it in me and wilt take it from me and return it to me in a life to come…. Blessed is the Returner of Souls to lifeless bodies."

For what, when lying down in bed the night before, was the man who says these words? A weary, depleted being, overwhelmed by the sensations of the day he has lived through—by its dispiriting waste of time, by the sins he has committed and that have saddened him, by all the people and things that have angered him. In this state he deposits his soul with God for safekeeping and receives it back the next morning, fresh, sparkling, and pure. A new day has come to the world, stripped of its soiled garments like a bedraggled eagle that molts its plumes and flies again.

And if this is so of all Jews, how much more so was it of me, rising early that morning in my own home. The night before I had said my bedtime prayers, laying down my soul with all that burdened it since the night after *Yom Kippur*—and now I rose a new man. My Lord! The soul that You did give me is pure. Another day had begun. Another world was calling. Might I again be the person I once was?

I felt reborn. My first twenty-four hour leave had left me invigorated. I said my morning prayers at sun-up, a Jew rising to greet his Maker; shouldered my pack; and went to the bus station. A morning chill was in the air. The station was coming to life. Drivers warmed the engines of parked buses and cleaned fogged windshields with shammy cloths. The food counters opened one by one. Yellow cheese sandwiches in plastic wrapping were stacked on trays. Not many passengers were waiting for buses. The only long line was for the 963 to Tiberias and Rosh Pina. It zigzagged between the handrails in several broken columns. Those on it were mostly soldiers. Some, spotless and clean-shaven, wore new uniforms with berets tucked neatly into shoulder loops above the insignia patches of their units.

Others were tankers dressed in their one-piece, fireproof suits, or bearded reservists in rumpled fatigues and an oddly gay assortment of stocking caps—orange, yellow, and green, as if to make sure they were not mistaken for disciplined troops. There were plain, ordinary soldiers too, about whom there was nothing special to say. Some, standing, were eating sandwiches bought at the counters. Others sat on the benches, flipping through the pages of yesterday's newspaper or catching up on their morning sleep, propped on packs bulging with items brought from home with their heads resting on the shoulders of their mates.

A group of loudly dressed teenagers was chatting at the front of the line. A woman stood off to one side, reciting the Morning Prayer from a small book while facing east toward the Temple Mount. An old man came by, rattling an alms box and calling out in flat tones, "Give! Give and be saved!" Another handed out little Psalters for good luck. An agitated couple ran toward our line. The husband was carrying two suitcases. "Has it left?" he asked. "The bus for Tiberias, has it left?"

"Has it left!" his wife mocked him. "Of course it has. Can't you see it's not here? We missed it by a minute. It's left, the bus has. We're always late. We're always missing buses."

"We're not late at all," the man with the suitcases said, glancing at a clock on the wall. "We're on time. It's those drivers for Tiberias. They always leave early. We'll wait for the next bus. That's the story of our lives. It's the story of everyone's life. There'll be another bus. There's bound to be. We'll get there."

No one took the trouble to inform them that they hadn't missed the bus at all. They didn't expect to be taken an interest in. After a while, an old fellow in a faded cap and a strange leather belt sat beside me and asked, whether for reassurance or to make small talk:

"This line, soldier, it's the line for Tiberias, isn't it?"

"Yes," I answered curtly, hoping to avoid a tedious conversation. "That's what the sign says. Tiberias."

"So you're going to Tiberias too," said the old man. "You know Tiberias? The tomb of Maimonides? Listen, soldier," he whispered in my ear. "Today is a celebration for me. What's so special, you ask? Why a celebration in the middle of the week? Listen, soldier—I'm finishing Maimonides' *Mishneh Torah* today. I've been studying it for three years, a chapter every day. There are a thousand chapters in it for the verse in The Song of Songs; *The thousand is yours, O Solomon.* And six more at the beginning and the end. That makes a thousand and six. That's the numerical value of the letters of *Mishneh Torah.* I'm finishing today, I am. I'll study the last chapter at the tomb."

The old fellow took out a small volume of Maimonides' code of laws and a plastic bag. He opened the bag and showed me its contents. "I've brought some dates for *havdalah* and a small bottle of wine. Old wine, I made it myself. I said the blessing over it at my grandson's circumcision. Held him on my knees, I did. Praise God, I was the godfather. Soldier, you're sure this is the line for Tiberias? Have a look," he whispered, his little eyes gleaming. He opened the volume. "These are the last two laws. They have to do with the wars of kings. You can read them if you like. Not me." He covered his eyes with his hand, as Jews do in the "Hear O Israel" prayer. "I have to finish at the tomb, not in the bus station. But you can read it. It's not your celebration."

I read:

> *Not to rule the world,*
> *And not to lord it over the Gentiles,*
> *And not to be favored among the nations,*
> *And not to eat, drink, and be merry,*
> *But to study the Torah and its wisdom*
> *Free of oppression and distraction,*
> *And to merit life in a World to Come*
> *That has neither war nor hunger,*
> *Nor envy nor contentiousness,*
> *But endless bounty for all,*
> *Amid which the pleasures of this life will be as dust,*
> *For the world will care only for the knowledge of God.*

I shut the book and handed it back.

"You've read it?" he asked, opening his eyes. He thumbed the volume and said, "And now, soldier, read a law from Chapter One. That's the Jewish way, to start again as soon as you finish. All endings are beginnings, because the *Torah* has no end." He shut his eyes and said, "I have to wait until Tiberias, but you—read now!"

What was I looking at?

"Read! Read!" he urged, sticking the book in front of me with his eyes still shut. I read:

"The foundation of all foundations and the pillar of all wisdom is the knowledge of a Prime Existent...."

"You've read it?" he asked. He opened his eyes and shut the book. "Today is a celebration for me. I'm finishing the last chapter. Soldier, you're sure this is the line for Tiberias?"

He took his bundle and went to look at the sign above the platform. Then he disappeared into the crowd.

Someone slapped me on the back. "Hey, what's doing? Did your company get a single twenty-four hour leave too?"

It was Moti, from Company 3. All I wanted was peace and quiet, not the scenes unleashed in my mind by the sight of him. But peace and quiet was not to be.

Moti and I had been on the same busload of soldiers from Jerusalem the night after *Yom Kippur*. Moti had sat with Shaya in the front of the bus. Shaya had been killed in the war. I had sat with Dov. Dov was killed too. All the way to Rosh Pina, Moti and Shaya had talked and laughed. Seeing Yisrael board the bus with a palm shoot, they had teased, "You've got to be kidding! Do you think we'll still be up on the Golan on the Feast of *Sukkot*? Aren't you taking this a bit too seriously? You should count on a shorter war."

The truth was that Yisrael's palm shoot amused us all. Little did we know that we would be eating *matzot* on the Golan the following *Pesach*.

"My father is a *Hasid*," Yisrael apologized. "He made me take a

49

palm shoot and a citron. He said his rabbi doesn't allow his *Hasidim* to travel without them after *Yom Kippur*. You never know."

"Give and be saved!" cried the old beggar, rattling his alms box. "Give and be saved!"

The bus for Tiberias hadn't pulled in yet. Several other buses came and went. "Everyone is waiting," the man with the suitcases told his wife. "It's bound to come." Unconvinced, she took an orange from her handbag, first peeling it slowly and then eating it segment by segment. Some passengers glanced irritably at their watches. The soldiers couldn't have cared less. They were in no hurry to get anywhere. Moti and I were silent. After a while he said:

"There's something I've been wanting to ask you. Maybe you remember. That first night at Camp Yiftach, when it was starting to get light and we were busy with the tanks, you came to say goodbye to Dov. He was saying the morning prayer and didn't want to stop, so he raised his voice and went on praying, as though it were meant for you, 'The soul that You did give me is pure. You did create it, You did form it, You did breathe it into me, You did sustain it in me, and You will take it from me and return it to me in a life to come...' You waved to him, climbed onto our tank, and asked me if I had any thread. You said that in basic training I was always the one stocked with everything. What on earth did you want to sew at such a time?"

He added:

"I don't know why that memory stuck in my mind. Perhaps because it was the last time I saw Dov. He was transferred at the last moment to another tank. I wanted to ask you about it, but we never met. I don't suppose you remember it. Not that it matters any more."

"Of course I remember," I said. "You really did have thread, although in the end it didn't do me any good. We had to work on the tanks in the dark. Everyone was shouting at once. 'Take these shells...Go bring some rifles... Don't forget binoculars ....We're short a crew member....' I crawled into the gunner's compartment to check the sights. We had an instructor in our tank course who always said,

'The first thing a gunner does is adjust his sights. You can't hit a thing before you do.' That whole night at Yiftach I kept hearing his voice. 'Gunner, adjust the sights! Gunner, adjust the sights!' As soon as there was enough light to make out a target, I went from tank to tank to look for a calibrator. Everyone laughed. 'Where do you think you're going to find a calibrator?' they said. 'We don't even have a pair of binoculars. Who has time for adjusting sights?' An officer shouted at me, 'Don't you understand that every second counts?' And then I remembered that Eran, my tank commander in the course, had taught me to adjust sights without a calibrator. You did it by making a cross over the muzzle of the gun with two threads dipped in grease to make them stick. I knew you were the only person in that madhouse who might have thread. And you did. Since the rest of the crew was too busy to help, I had to do it all by myself. I made the cross, ran to the loader's compartment, removed the firing pin from the breech so as to see the length of the barrel, ran to the gunner's compartment, put the gun on a target, and ran back to the loader's compartment to set the cross on it. All that was left was to return to the gunner's compartment, see how much the sights had moved, and correct the deviation. Just then an officer yelled at Roni, 'Driver, get going! What are you waiting for?' 'I need one more minute,' I said. 'Another minute and I'm done.' 'Not another second!' the officer yelled. 'You should be up on the Heights already! Don't you realize what's happening?' Roni put the tank in gear, the gun moved, and that was the end of the adjustment. It was a crying shame, because I was almost finished. I replaced the firing pin, climbed into the gunner's compartment, and drove off to the war with unadjusted sights like everyone else. Gidi said to me, 'Don't worry. You'll make the adjustment when we get there.' He thought it was going to be the Six Day War all over again. Another minute was all I needed...."

"That was tough luck," Moti agreed. "Who knows if that minute didn't make the difference."

We lapsed into thought. The old beggar rattled his box. "Give! Give and be saved!"

The man with the suitcases said to his wife: "It looks like you're right for once. We really did miss the bus. But maybe it's just as well. Every delay is a chance to make hay, as they say. It's all God's will."

The woman shrugged.

"What do you know?" the man with the suitcases said. "What does anyone know?"

Chapter six

The Sea of Galilee appeared ahead of us. Then the bus swung left at the Tsemach junction and the serenely green water was on our right. It wove its usual spell on me. I stared at it, trying to figure out what this was. Perhaps Miriam's well in its depths. Most of the passengers were asleep. One was singing quietly. I recognized the melody. Then I made out the words. They belonged to a familiar hymn.

> *Yea, every day I wait and pray,*
> *My heart and soul so curious*
> *To journey to that holy place,*
> *The city of Tiberias.*

Unable to resist, I joined in:

> *O pleasant is the sight of it,*
> *O goodly are its strands,*
> *The lake, the hills, the walls around,*
> *'Twixt which the city stands.*

Startled, the voice broke off. I turned and spotted the old
fellow with the dates and the strange belt in a seat by the rear door.
He saw me, waved, and resumed singing, his eyes shut and his head
bobbing as in prayer:

> *O'er the mountains, where he rests,*
> *The giant of his age, I spy*
> *Enshrined upon its sacred ground,*
> *The tomb of Yohanan Ben-Zakkai.*

> *And there beside him also lies*
> *The master of all commentaries,*
> *A second Moses, wisdom's prince,*
> *Our faith's great guide, Maimonides.*

I was a boy in the *Talmud Torah* when I learned that song.
Although we didn't take many school trips, we did go every year,
between *Pesach* and *Shavuot*, to the holy sites of Tiberias and Mount
Meron. This was always preceded by great excitement. A week in
advance our teacher would tell us wondrous tales about Tiberias and
its rabbis and about Safed and its kabbalists. Once he related:

"Rabbi Meir the Miracle Worker is buried in Tiberias. His
tomb is covered by a large dome and looks out over the lake, and
many sorely afflicted men and women come there to give alms and
cry, 'O God of Meir, answer me!' And indeed, they are answered. And
if you want to know why Rabbi Meir is called 'the Miracle Worker,'
I'll tell you.

"Rabbi Haninah ben Teradyon was one of the ten saintly
martyrs put to death by the Romans for disobeying their ban on
studying the *Torah*. Once, when his master, Rabbi Yosi ben Kisma,
fell ill, Rabbi Haninah paid a call on him. Rabbi Yosi said, 'Haninah,
my brother! Do you not know that the Romans have been appointed
from Heaven to rule the world? How else could they continue to exist
after destroying God's Temple and burning His shrine and decimating
His people and killing the worthiest of them? And yet I have been

told that you persist in defying them and gathering students around you with a *Torah* scroll on your knees!'

"Rabbi Haninah replied, 'I count on the mercy of Heaven.'

"Rabbi Yosi said to him, 'I am speaking sense and you talk of Heaven's mercy! I fear that you and the *Torah* will be burned together.'

"'Master,' Haninah asked, 'have I a place in Paradise?'

"Rabbi Yosi said, 'Why, what have you done?'

"'Once,' said Haninah, 'I confused some money raised for a *Purim* feast with alms collected for the poor and I gave it to them.'

"Rabbi Yosi said to him, 'Your place in Paradise will be next to mine and my fate will be yours.'

"It is said that not many days went by before Rabbi Yosi ben Kisma passed away. The prominent Romans all attended his funeral and a stirring eulogy was given. On their way back from the graveyard they found Haninah ben Teradyon with students gathered round and a *Torah* scroll on his knees. He and his wife were sentenced to die at the stake, while his daughter was condemned to a life of shame. He was taken and wrapped in a *Torah* scroll. A pyre of branches was made, a fire was lit, and pads of wool soaked in water were laid on his chest to make his death a slow one.

"'Father, has it come to this?' his daughter cried out.

"Haninah said to her, 'Were I being burned alone, it would go hard with me. But since I am being burned with the *Torah*, He who avenges it will avenge me.'

"'Rabbi,' his disciples asked him, 'what do you see?'

"Haninah said, 'I see the parchment of the *Torah* scroll burning and its letters released into the air.'

"They said, 'Then you, too, open your mouth and swallow fire and be released!'

"He said to them, 'Let a man's life be taken by its Giver and not by himself.'

"Hearing these words, the stoker of the fire said to him, 'Rabbi, if I stoke the flames higher and remove the wet pads, will you take me with you to Paradise?'

"Rabbi Haninah said, 'Yes.'

"'Swear!'

"Rabbi Haninah swore. Then the stoker stoked the flames and removed the pads and Haninah ben Teradyon's soul departed at once. As it did so he blessed his fate and said, *'He is the Rock, His ways are perfect; for all His ways are judgment.'*

"His wife, who was standing by, continued the verse and said, *'A God of truth and without iniquity.'*

"And his daughter finished it, adding, *'Just and right is He.'*

"Then the stoker leaped into the flames.

"There came forth from Heaven the proclamation, 'Rabbi Haninah ben Teradyon and the stoker are welcomed in the World to Come!'

"When Rabbi Judah the Prince heard this, he wept and said: 'Some labor for years to merit Paradise and some gain entry in a moment.'"

Our teacher added:

"And so Rabbi Haninah was burned at the stake and his daughter was sent to a brothel in Rome. But Haninah had another daughter, Bruriah, the wife of Rabbi Meir. She pleaded with her husband to ransom her sister and he took a sack of gold coins and went to Rome.

"In Rome, Rabbi Meir went to the doorman of the brothel and said, 'Take these coins and let me have Haninah's daughter.'

"'I'm afraid,' the doorman said.

"'Take these coins,' said Rabbi Meir. "Keep half for yourself and give half to your superiors.'

"'The doorman said, 'I'm still afraid.'

"'If you're caught,' Rabbi Meir told him, 'you need only call out, "O God of Meir, answer me," and you'll be saved.'

"And that is what happened. The doorman was caught and sentenced to be hanged. On the gallows he called out the words Rabbi Meir taught him and he was saved."

Our teacher also told us stories about Rabbi Shimon bar Yochai and his son Rabbi Elazar, and about Rabbi Yitzhak Ashkenazi of Safed, known as the Ari, the Holy Lion, who once said to his disciples on a Sabbath eve: "Come, let us go welcome the Sabbath in Jerusalem." "First we must ask our families," his disciples replied. Then the Holy Lion grieved greatly and struck his hands and declared that if only his disciples had set out with him in perfect faith at once, the Messiah would have come. Now the chance had been lost.

The day of our school outing was a fine one, not too hot and not too cold. We rose early and took a bus from the *Talmud Torah* to Tiberias. Dov sat next to me. We spent all day riding the bus and visiting different places. It was nearly sunset when we reached the Sea of Galilee. As it came into view our teacher asked if anyone knew a song about it. The boys in the bus broke excitedly into one folk song after another, starting each new one before the old one was finished. When they had run out of songs, there was silence.

The teacher asked if anyone knew another song. I raised a hesitant hand. The teacher called on me. I knew a song about Tiberias and the Sea of Galilee, I said, but it was not like the ones we had sung. It was a synagogue hymn.

"So what?" said the teacher. "A song is a song!" He called for silence and I went to the front of the bus and sang:

> *Yea, every day I wait and pray,*
> *My heart and soul so curious*
> *To journey to that holy place,*
> *The city of Tiberias.*

I sang on, proud to know so many stanzas by heart. But after two more of them, I saw no one was listening. I broke off and some boys struck up a comic ditty that they had invented about our driver. Our teacher asked me where the song came from. It was, I said, a hymn I had learned from my teacher, Mr. Revach, who was said to have been a famous hymn composer in Morocco. Since he also kept a small vegetable garden in the immigrant shantytown of Beit Mazmil, he had been asked to teach gardening as well as liturgy.

I returned to my seat. Dov tried to salve my hurt feelings by asking for another stanza. I sang:

> *The pure of heart will there find peace*
> *At night when they lie down,*
> *Each one of them so close to God*
> *In that most holy town.*

Through the windows of the bus we could see the white dome of the tomb of Rabbi Meir the Miracle Worker. Dov asked me if I remembered the story of Rabbi Haninah ben Teradyon and the *Torah* scroll. I said I did.

"There's something strange about it," Dov said.

"What's that?"

Dov said, "What could Rabbi Yosi have been thinking of when Haninah asked 'Have I a place in Paradise?' and he answered 'Why, what have you done?'" He hesitated and continued: "One possible explanation is that Rabbi Yosi was asking Haninah if he had ever done a bad deed and Haninah told him that he had mistakenly given money to the poor. To which Rabbi Yosi replied, 'Nevertheless, your place in Paradise will be next to mine.'"

Dov stopped to think. Then he said:

"I don't think that's right. I think Rabbi Yosi was asking Haninah if he had ever done a *good* deed. Haninah's answer was that he had once confused money raised for a *Purim* feast with alms collected for the poor, and that he gave the entire sum to the poor to be on the safe side."

Dov paused and went on: "But if that's what Rabbi Yosi was asking, what kind of question was it? Didn't he know Haninah was risking his life by teaching the *Torah*? Wasn't that the best deed anyone could have done?"

I had no answer. Dov said: "From this we learn that there are different kinds of good deeds. There are those that everyone knows about, performed by great men at great moments, and there are those that seem trivial, performed in the ordinary moments of ordinary days. And it's the second kind that earn us a place in Paradise."

The old man behind me was still singing:

Yea, every day I wait and pray,
My heart and soul so curious
To journey to that holy place,
The city of Tiberias.

The old fellow came toward me up the aisle. His volume of Maimonides lay open in his hand. There was something he wanted to tell me. I was ready to listen now, too, but just then the bus pulled into Tiberias. The passengers scolded him for blocking the aisle and he got off without telling me what he wanted to. All I heard him say was:

"*Wherefore doth a living man complain*? Be glad you're alive."

The bus emptied out. Only a few soldiers stayed on until Rosh Pina. Some women from the Soldiers Aid Society were standing by the curb there, handing out chocolate cookies and coffee in plastic cups. Someone was selling zippers that could be attached to army boots. The latest invention. We waited for a lift outside the PX. One of us stood by the road to stop a car while the others sat against their packs. After a while a small car pulled up.

The driver was a woman. "If you're heading for the Golan," she told us, "I can take you as far as the quarry in Nafah."

I wondered what business she had in the quarry at Nafah. Four of us, Moti, myself, and two infantry soldiers, piled into the little car with our full packs, our rifles, and our muddy boots. The woman said no more. The two infantry soldiers fell asleep right away. Moti took out a book. I stared out the window with a queasy feeling. I was as tense as a bowstring the moment before the musician draws his bow.

We were taking the same road that we had taken the night after *Yom Kippur*, traveling on our tank treads. Everything now reminded me of something then.

It was raining. The tall eucalyptus trees at the north end of Rosh Pina were dripping wet. The car smelled sharply of them and of the wet leaves trampled by the boots of the soldiers. The smell was familiar. It carried me back into the past. We were standing in our tankers suits, a group of us, beneath a eucalyptus tree in Camp Yiftach, crumbling the pungent leaves in our fingers while waiting for the divisional adjutant to call out each time a tank came from the repair shop: "I need a gunner! I need a loader! I need a driver!" This time we knew what was in store for us. All around us the two-way radios in divisional headquarters were spewing out voices from the tanks fighting above. We didn't bother to listen. We had already been there.

The smell of the eucalyptus trees made me think of the glances that passed between us as we waited to see who would volunteer and who would avoid the others' eyes. Although we all saw through it, no one said a word. There was one man who hadn't seen action yet. He was a gunner who had reached Yiftach too late for the first wave of tanks. Now a gunner was needed. Everyone looked at him. "We've been there," the eyes said. "It's your turn." But the man looked away. Moti was next in line. I was after him. He jerked his head at the man and clenched his lips. I watched in silence as he went off to join a new crew. Then I went too. The man stayed behind. Years later, when I sometimes ran into him, he still couldn't look me in the eyes. I knew he wanted me to forgive him. It wasn't something I could do.

We were heading downhill toward the bridge over the Jordan. The woman appeared to know the way. I supposed she was from the area. By now Moti had fallen asleep too. So many memories were running through my mind that I couldn't keep them apart. Here, at this bend, Sriel had waved a cheerful goodbye to me from the loader's compartment of his tank. He was still dressed for synagogue, having been too busy stacking shells to put on tanker's overalls. That was how his body was found, dressed in its best for the best of all worlds.

He had been a natty dresser at the *yeshiva* too, even on ordinary days. Or was I just imagining that?

I stared out the window. It wasn't easy. But even if I shut my eyes, I still saw everything. We were almost at the bridge. There, by those bushes on the right, next to that tree, we had passed a mechanized infantry battalion sprawled on its packs. A battalion from another division had reached Camp Yiftach before it and made off with its APCs. The battalion commander was furious. How could you walk away with someone's personnel carriers? What kind of army was that? He didn't want to miss the war. Who knew how long it would last?

We took the last turn before the bridge. This was where Tzion's tank had stalled. The entire column had come to a halt. Commanders jumped from their tanks to help. We used the time to chat with friends. We didn't get beyond small talk. No one thought it was the last time we would ever speak to Shmuel, Dov, or Shaya.

The car crossed the bridge. The Jordan flowed below. Instinctively I glanced at the sky. From here we had watched an airplane fall. Gidi and Roni had argued whose it was. Gidi was right. It was ours. That our planes too could be shot down was a novel concept.

Beyond the bridge the queasy feeling grew worse. Soon we would come to Nafah, to the quarry, to the Tapline road, to the black rocks, to the mud huts with their cattle pens. This was the route we had taken. The infantry soldiers were awake. We passed the quarry. I needed to talk to someone and considered waking Moti. I didn't realize I was talking already.

"You see that bare patch? That was our jumping-off point for the attack on Hushniya. The CO assembled all the tanks in the middle of the night. One force led while the other covered it from the ridgeline. We were in the cover." I pointed at some ground and said, "The brigade second, Avihu, had his tank there. He was a brave man. We were on the hill up ahead. 2-A was over there and 2 was next to it. The sun was in our eyes. We couldn't see. Suddenly all hell broke loose. The Syrian tanks had set up an ambush during the night. They were there." I pointed. "They were firing from close range. We were so close that one of their tanks filled my whole periscope. We kept shooting all the time. Eli, my loader, was drenched in sweat. He was falling off his feet. He was working harder than any of us, loading shells, bending down for more, freeing them from their clips, ramming them into the breech. Our tanks were being hit. We knew who was in each of them. They were burning like bonfires. The Syrians were picking us off one by one. We changed positions and went on firing."

I fell silent, aware that the whole car was listening. The driver pulled over and asked me to show her where the covering force had stood. We got out and walked over the rocky ground. "We came this way," I said, leading the way without stopping to think. I was practically running up the hill. "This is where we dug in. The company commander had his tank there. Avihu was over there. His gun was aimed in that direction."

"Could you show me exactly where?" the woman asked.

I hesitated. The black rocks all looked the same. I stepped from one to another. All at once I pointed to a thorn bush:

"Here," I said. "Right here."

I glanced at the two infantry soldiers. I could tell they thought I was bluffing. I didn't care. I was used to it. But the woman seemed to believe me. She was staring at the ground strangely. After a while she said, "Let's go back to the car."

I lingered for a last look, as if hoping to find something. An object was lying on the ground. I recognized it. Everybody watched me pick it up. It was half of a 75-mm. binoculars.

"Here," I said. "This was Avihu's. It was smashed. This was the place."

The woman put the broken binoculars to her eye and stared through it. I asked what made her so interested in the battle of Nafah quarry.

"I'm from Kibbutz Kfar Giladi," she said. "The quarry was ours. Avihu was its manager."

We started back for the car.

"He was my brother," she said, as though to herself.

Chapter seven

Not all times and days are the same. There are long days and short days, full times and empty ones. There are hours that go by like years and years that pass like hours, interminable moments and lifetimes like a fleeting dream.

My first leave was over. I had been given twenty-four hours and they were up. How much of that other, parallel time passed between leaving and rejoining my unit on the Golan Heights, I couldn't say. My last lift brought me from the square in Kuneitra to battalion headquarters. From there I radioed my company. "Welcome back," Hanan said. It was good to hear his voice. He didn't wait to hang up before sending the next gunner home. The time was too precious to waste even a minute of it. He put me back on the roster and I waited for a supply truck that would drop me off at the company bivouac. It was parked outside the battalion kitchen. Soldiers were loading it with field rations. A staff sergeant was fighting with the battalion cook to add more cans and fresh food. The cook wanted to hold back as much as he could.

I asked Marciano, the battalion quartermaster, to let me know when the truck was leaving and went to the communications tent to try to place a call home. That was something you did automatically whenever you were in battalion headquarters. In our bivouac in Tel Hiros we had no telephone, only a two-way radio. Every few weeks a mobile phone crew came around. That was always a special day. We kept getting back in line and phoning everyone we knew until the crew moved on.

I stepped into the tent. An officer was on duty at the switchboard. Little orange and yellow bulbs blinked on and off. He had a receiver pressed to his ear and was talking into another while plugging and unplugging wires. He gave me a hesitant glance, then took off the earphones, left the switchboard, and came over.

"You don't know who I am," he said. "I'm sure you don't remember me. But I remember you. It's not something a person forgets. I never thought I'd see you again. I had no idea how you came out of the war. I didn't know if you were still in the battalion or even alive."

He leveled his gaze at me and said: "I owe you an apology. I'll tell you why. I was the first person you ran into when you came down to Yiftach for another tank. You were bushed. Your eyes were bloodshot. You were smeared with soot. Your tankers' suit was filthy and shapeless and you were holding an Uzi without a strap. And while you looked sane enough, you said that your company had lost most of its tanks and the Syrians were at Nafah, knocking out our armor and shooting down our planes with missiles. You didn't stop talking. I was on duty at the entrance to the mess hall with another man and we were grinning. We didn't believe a word you said. You didn't notice us making signs that you were shell-shocked. We had heard about such things. 'Soldier,' I said, 'have a cold drink and calm down. Tanks don't burn so easily. And planes don't just fall from the sky. Relax. The war will be over in a few days.' It was too much for us to take in."

He silenced a nervous buzz from the switchboard and went on:

"You and another tanker asked if you could get something to eat

64

in the mess hall. We told you it wasn't possible because we had orders to admit only soldiers stationed on the base. That was the truth. We'd been informed that the tank crews had their own rations. I can't tell you how ashamed I felt afterwards. I wish I could take those words back. God knows what you had been through."

The switchboard buzzed again. A yellow bulb was blinking. The communications officer went back to it.

He was right: I didn't remember him. But I would never forget being told that Eli and I couldn't eat in the mess hall of our own base. "You have your own rations," we were told. Hungry and exhausted, we let ourselves be scolded for leaving our rations in a burning tank so that we could look for another one to fight in. The soldiers from the base kept filing in, talking and paying us no attention. Finally, the captain of the mechanized infantry company came along. His men were still sitting on their packs. They had been told by the major that this wasn't a war for them and he didn't want them getting killed for no good reason. The captain saw us standing there, too tired to feel angry or insulted, and took us to the officers' mess.

Marciano was shouting: "Hey you—tank guy! Where did you go? I told you to stay put. I'm out of here. Now!"

I climbed onto the supply truck. It was a short drive to my company. We were bivouacked at Tel Hiros, at the near end of the Syrian bulge, in four tents and a tin shack. One tent was for the officers and the others were for the crews, two crews to a tent. The rumor was that two more tanks with crews would be joining us from the brigade. When we weren't standing watch, we spent our time in the tents. It was too windy and rainy to go out, which we did only to service the tanks and heat our battle rations in the shack. Six or seven men could squeeze into it. Half the space was taken up by a noisy generator. Hanan spent hours working on it every day, oiling it and refilling its fuel tank and tinkering with its wires and banging with a hammer, all to no avail. Something always went wrong with it.

In the shack's other half we heated the cans of peas and beans brought by the supply truck. Most of our talk around the gas burner had to do with rumors of our demobilization. Everyone had heard a different version. The one thing they all had in common was that there was no truth in any of them. Now and then you heard an intelligent conversation, usually started by something someone had read. Not a day went by without Itzik asking me whether the *Talmud* said when the Messiah would come. He was sure we had just fought the war of Gog and Magog. Told by me that I didn't know, he asked for a *Talmudic* story. He liked listening to them. I told him the ones I remembered, especially those with happy endings. Sometimes others gathered around and listened too.

Now and then someone read us a letter from his small son or showed us a drawing sent him by his daughter. We never talked about the war. Everyone kept his memories to himself. There was one man who upended an empty ammunition crate in a corner of the shack, covered it with a cloth, and stood writing all day long, hunched protectively over the paper. There was much speculation about him. Some said he was writing poetry; others that he was drawing picture postcards for the children who had written us care of The Soldiers Aid Society; still others, that he was composing anti-war protests to send to the heads of state. Alfonso thought he was keeping a diary about everything that had happened to us. That way, someone might believe us one day.

The days went by. A third of them passed in sleep, a third servicing the tanks, and a third waiting for the supply truck from battalion headquarters. Marciano always came with it. He brought spare parts for the tanks, fresh tankers' suits, and laundered rags made from old fatigues. We wrapped the rags around the rods, fitted together in seven sections, with which we cleaned and greased the gun barrels at night and wiped them dry in the morning.

Kimmel, the spic-and-span battalion adjutant with the eyeglasses, always accompanied Marciano. He brought mail, newspapers, PX items, and sometimes checks from National Insurance. He also brought regards from the companies bivouacked at Tel Antar and Tel Grin, and the latest scuttlebutt from battalion headquarters about when and by whom we would be relieved and what would happen to us when we were. Each time he arrived, Zada asked about his baby chicks. Zada owned a hatchery and had no one to look after it, because his partner was in the army too. No matter how many times he gave his wife instructions over the phone, she couldn't follow them. Many chicks had died already. Kimmel listened attentively, took a pen and a small red notepad from his pocket, and jotted everything down. Then he slapped Zada on the back and said a few encouraging words. Once he brought him a check. It was compensation for ten chicks.

The rest of the day was taken up with unpacking and arranging the new supplies. Sometimes we received shipments of fresh fruit, candies, and cigarettes. Sometimes there were surprises. The non-smokers traded their cigarettes for chocolates, which they kept to bring to their children on their next leave. Men swapped soiled uniforms for fresh ones, read their mail five or six times, and wrote long letters in reply.

One of us, a student at the Hebrew University, struggled to keep up with the course work sent him from Jerusalem. With a bit of luck, he said, he might salvage the semester. The university refused to postpone his exams. He would have to manage, he was told. Serious institutions of learning didn't make individual exceptions. This was a decision of the university senate.

Tzion had got his hands on a small volume of the *Talmud*, the tractate of *Bava Batra*, and he and two others soldiers held a daily study session. Each tried to remember what he had learned in his *yeshiva*. When their memories failed they reminisced about their teachers, since discussing learned men, the Sages said, is tantamount to learning. It gave them something to look forward to.

Alfonso, the loader of 2-B, spent his time engrossed in a fat Spanish book, his face buried in its pages while he listened to Schubert and Mozart on his transistor radio through earphones. All we saw of him, he said, was his body. His spirit was somewhere else.

Two crews played cards around the clock. And there were men who sat around doing nothing, killing time until they were demobilized.

The days were short at Tel Hiros. The December cold was bitter, and lights and fires were forbidden. We ate an early supper, retired to our tents, bundled up in our windbreakers and army blankets, and tried to sleep until it was time to stand watch in the driving rain. One crew, a gunner, loader, and tank commander, refused to leave their tent for anything but guard duty. They also refused to say why. They wouldn't even join us for the banquets we sometimes prepared from our rations—mackerel fried in its oil, sautéed canned meat with baked beans, and grapefruit sections for dessert. When the supply truck arrived, they'd take their share and retire to their tent. There they sat on their cots, slicing the meat on the lid of its can and eating it cold on bread. When it was time for their watch they took their rifles and trooped off without a word. At sunrise they serviced their tank and went back to their tent. They took no part in our morning calisthenics. Asked a question by Hanan, they either nodded or shook their heads.

Hanan left them alone. We all knew that the war had done funny things to people. They even stayed in their tent when the major came to announce with a flourish the start of the twenty-four hour leaves, and they turned down our invitation to join the draw. They trusted us, they said, to let them know if any of them was the lucky winner. According to Zada, their tank had been hit at Khan Arnaba. All of them abandoned it except for the driver, who was trapped by the hatch, after which they stopped talking. Sasha, however, said that Zada was confusing their story with that of a different tank at Nafah. No one bothered to ask the men themselves, and I shut my eyes while Zada and Sasha argued and thought of Dov. Sometimes I couldn't think of anything else. His tank had left Yiftach on the afternoon of the first day and was hit on its way to Nafah quarry. Or so I had been told. But what had happened to him? How could nobody know? What tank were Zada and Sasha arguing about?

Chapter eight

Three weeks had gone by since my leave and I was counting the days till the next one. Winter had arrived and with it the realization that we would be lighting *Hanukkah* candles on the Golan. One cloudy afternoon, a mobilized civilian car drove up to our bivouac. Three young lieutenants climbed out of it. They were wearing freshly pressed uniforms with war ribbons on their chests and shiny bars on their shoulders. Hanan was in his old fatigues. We never saw him with his lieutenant's bars. One night he had assembled us, held out a handful of war ribbons received from the adjutant's office, and said, "Take your pick." We each took a ribbon and stuck it in our packs. That same evening he informed us that we had all been promoted to corporal. He had asked the operations chief why and was told that anyone living through a war like this one deserved to be more than a private.

The officers who got out of the car wanted to know where our company commander was. We told them to look in the shack, where Hanan was crouched over the generator, trying to get it to work. He went with them to the command tent. After a while he came out, made the rounds of the other tents, and announced that the visitors wanted to talk to us. They were from corps headquarters in Tel Aviv. One was an Intelligence debriefer, one a military historian, and one an army psychologist. They were documenting the experiences of soldiers in the war.

"Please," Hanan said almost imploringly. "Try to cooperate. It's an order from above. Let's get it over with."

The crews straggled from their tents. Alfonso came with his Spanish book and his transistor. Tzion carried his volume of *Bava Batra*, opened to the laws of property rights. The crew of 2-B brought its cards and continued playing on its way to the command tent. Sasha, stubble-cheeked as always, his long hair hanging to his shoulders, wore the yellow stocking cap with the red pompom that he never took off. He laughed grimly when he spied the clean-shaven officers, their lieutenant's bars gleaming. Each held a file holder. "Go tell them our experiences," Sasha said.

They were from Tel Aviv. They had come to listen to us and take notes. They thought wars were the way the books and Intelligence reports described them. Once I had thought that too. No doubt they would ask us why we had done this and not that, such as execute a flanking movement or call for air or artillery support. They had questions for us? *We* had questions for them. Perhaps they could tell us what had happened on that second day at Nafah. Who was shooting at whom? And what made the Syrians halt their advance? Why hadn't they marched on Tiberias? And why had our tanks been mothballed in the depot without their equipment? Let them explain to us how we were supposed to fight in tanks that had no binoculars or calibrators and had to be started with auxiliary chargers. And maybe someone knew why Menachem's company had been marooned at Wasit Junction without maps or radio communication while enemy fire rained down on it. Exactly what did the young officers from Tel Aviv think we were going to help them to understand? We didn't understand the first thing ourselves.

"Men, let's get it over with," Hanan begged. We gathered around his tank. The officers stood facing us, hands on hips. We exchanged mocking looks. Although he was doing his best to keep us in line, you could see Hanan was on our side. The officer in the middle explained that each of us would relate his memories of a single day of the war during a span of twenty-four consecutive hours. We had nothing to be afraid of. We wouldn't be asked for our names or serial numbers. Everything would be kept confidential. While we were waiting to be interviewed, the debriefer handed out forms and requested that we fill them out by listing the number and types of shells we had fired; from what ranges; with what firing orders; and with what damage to the enemy's tanks and unarmored vehicles. The army also wished to know how many cannon rounds had been needed to hit each target; how many machine gun bullets we had averaged with each burst; what the average speed of each tank had been; and the radio communications we had received. Also, how many of us used our field dressing; did it stop the bleeding; and various other things. We were handed pencils and forms. Each form came with four thin carbon copies that rustled when you handled them. It was divided into lines, columns and boxes.

Next came a talk by the psychologist. He spoke slowly and deliberately, pausing frequently to gauge our reactions. He must have been taught to do that in some course. He introduced himself by his first name and said that he was in no hurry and had all the time in the world. The important thing was to skip no detail, no matter how small: what we had done at each moment, and what we had felt and thought, and how the wounded had reacted, and who had evacuated them, and had we been afraid, and what had we done to cope with it, and had we prayed and what had we said in our prayers. We could even tell him our dreams.

"Don't worry, baby!" Zada called out. "None of us is whacko."

"I'd say that's a question of definition," Sasha whispered.

The debriefer invited us into the shack by threes. I was with Elhanan and Shlomo. We were all *yeshiva* students. Elhanan had been Hanan's driver when Hanan was a platoon leader. Shlomo was the gunner of Vagman, the battalion's second-in-command. The debriefer sat in the middle of a table before a disorderly pile of forms and papers. He looked tense. The psychologist was on his right; he had nothing in front of him but a glass of water and sat with his chin in his hand, studying each soldier. The historian sat on the left with a neat notebook in which he occasionally jotted something down.

Hanan crouched by the generator, banging it to turn it off.

I sat across the table.

"What day of the war do you want to tell us about, soldier?" asked the debriefer without looking up at me.

"The second day," I said. "From the morning of the second day to the morning of the third."

He wrote something on a sheet of paper, glanced up at me, and asked for the exact dates.

I didn't understand the question. "Dates?" I said. "It was the second day! The second day of the war." How many second days were there?

We manned our tanks on the night after *Yom Kippur*. The next morning we moved up to the Golan, toward Wasit Junction. Late that afternoon we were told to head for Nafah in a hurry. There we saw our first burned-out tanks. At dawn on the second day we drove into the ambush in the quarry. What dates was he talking about?

"I'm sorry," he apologized. "We're obliged to record the date." He consulted a pocket diary and wrote something. "Go on," he said.

"One minute," said the psychologist. He told me to speak slowly and to leave nothing out. It didn't matter how unimportant it seemed. Everything was important.

The historian said nothing.

I plunged straight in and talked without stopping for breath. The officers sat with blank faces across from me, taking notes from time to time. Although I kept looking at them, I couldn't tell if they believed me. They were careful to show no emotion. All they did was take notes while I talked.

About how tanks were being hit all around us, 1-B, 1-D, and 3-A. And about how we knew the men in each tank because we had all come up together from below, and had studied together at the *yeshiva* and argued about knotty passages in the *Talmud* and the philosophical subtleties of Maimonides, and had been in boot camp together and stood all night on the parade grounds putting on our battle gear in the dark while being shouted at by Sergeant Gavrieli, and had pushed ourselves to the limit on a stretcher march through the plowed fields near Givat Olga, gritting our teeth and keeping each other going, and had circled the camp on the run with our rifles over our heads, hazed by a squad instructor who signaled each new round with the little finger of a hand kept on his hip, and had been sent for tank training when someone at General Staff decided—much to the displeasure of those of us who had dreamed of being paratroopers—that the next war would be fought by armor, and had trained in the sands of Sinai, and had been called up together on *Yom Kippur* and sent to the tank depot in Camp Yiftach.

I sat facing the three officers and tried to talk coherently. I knew that was important. I just couldn't stop everything from flashing through my mind and distracting me. I shut my eyes and saw Shmuel. The driver of 3-A, he knew by heart every line of the *Shulhan Aruch*. At the *yeshiva* he had always been our prayer leader. When our column was held up, approaching the Jordan bridge, he had stuck out his head from his tank and told Itzik he was glad he was going to war right after *Yom Kippur*, still pure from prayer and confession. I said to the officers:

"I was in the gunner's compartment. I knew every man in every tank that was hit.

"There was no time to think of them, though. Or of ourselves. There was only time to aim and shoot. We were in a war. I struggled to focus on the sights. The Syrian tanks were on the ridge across from us. The attacking force below us was close to them, moving up the wadi toward Hushniya. We were covering it. I had to make sure I wasn't shooting at our own tanks. Generally, the Syrian tanks were easy to identify. They had rounder turrets and a different gun. But now everything was confused and the sun was blinding me. And there wasn't a second to spare. A second could mean life or death. I had to trust Gidi, who was spotting. But although he had his head out of the turret, he couldn't see any better than I could. I aimed high, as we were taught to do in maneuvers, and corrected myself by lowering the range. A Syrian tank burst into flames. 'Direct hit!' I cried and swiveled the gun to the next tank. I fired at the same trajectory and hit that too. I was gaining confidence. Gidi spotted some trucks of Syrian infantry and opened up with the machine gun. It was hard to see where the rounds landed. A truck began to burn.

Syrian shells were coming closer. Two tanks were hit on our right. Eli thought a Syrian tank was on our flank and firing from there. Gidi couldn't spot it and ordered us to maintain covering fire straight ahead. But the sun was blinding me again and we had been in one place too long. On maneuvers we were taught to change positions often. We should have done it already. Gidi wouldn't give the order, though. We were the only tank in the covering force still firing and we had to stay where we were. 'Gunner, fire!' he called over the intercom. 'Fire!' He no longer gave a range or shell. Eli had been told to load whatever he could grab first. 'Hollow charge in the breech!' he shouted, ramming it home. 'Squash nose in the barrel!' I took aim as best I could through the observation slat. We were at such close range that the target filled the whole periscope. I didn't bother using it. The slat was enough. I fired. A shell landed near us. Gidi spotted the tank on our flank. I swiveled the gun. The sun was in my eyes. The lense of the periscope was a white glare. I had to find it. Please, God! Just for a second. Just this once. I strained to see. There it was. 'Firing squash nose!' I called. 'We're in its sights!' Gidi shouted. 'Gunner, combat range, fire! Driver, back up, quick! Gunner, pray!' I could barely hear him over the intercom. I fired and yelled, 'You pray too, Gidi!' 'I don't know how to!' he called back."

I prayed as hard as I could. *I beseech Thee, O Lord, save us.*

After we manned the tanks at Yiftach the night after *Yom Kippur*, Shaya went from tank to tank. When he reached our tank, he called to me and Roni. We were stacking shells. Roni was on the ground, bending over an ammunition crate and hurriedly handing its contents to me. From time to time he caught a finger in the clips and bled. A passing quartermaster threw us a rag and told us to wipe the blood off the shells. It brought bad luck, he said. I stood on the turret, taking the shells and passing them down to Eli in the hull. All you could see of him was the fringes of his ritual undershirt. Shaya had come to remind us to pray. "Do it before we head out," he said.

We were three *yeshiva* boys in one tank crew, Roni, Eli, and I. Our regular commander hadn't made it to the base. His place was taken by Gidi, a reservist fresh from six years in Los Angeles. He had forgotten a great deal, had never used the new tank helmets, and was unfamiliar with the crew and the communications system. But he would learn on the job, he said.

"Don't worry," he told us. "I cut my teeth on the Six Day War. There'll be plenty of time before we fire our first shot. We'll get organized at the jumping-off point. We'll get orders and maps and communications codes and adjust the sights. And by then I'll remember how to buckle a commander's helmet and give firing orders. Just stack as many shells as you can, especially hollow charges. I don't trust the squash noses. I never did."

He was assembling the machine gun when he heard Shaya tell us to pray. Looking up from the barrel, he said: "You guys better know who you're going to war with. I'm an atheist."

That was long ago. Before the war.

"Combat range! Fire!" I let loose a shell. Roni shifted into reverse. There was a loud boom. The periscope jumped and hit me in the eye.

When I described that boom to the three officers, I felt the pain in my eye all over again. Now, as I write about it years later, it's back once more, in the same place it was then, right over the brow. I continued: "The tank was rocking back and forth. The periscope hit me again, this time in the shoulder. I didn't know what had happened. 'Crew, we've been hit! Abandon tank!' That was Gidi's voice in the earphones of my helmet that was a size too small. It had to be his, because only the intercom was working. The radio had been out of commission for a while. I grabbed the strapless Uzi that I had taken at the last minute from Camp Yiftach on the night after *Yom Kippur.*"

A brigade quartermaster had blocked the entrance to the armory. No one, he said, was taking weapons without first filling out a form in duplicate. He didn't care if there was a war, he wasn't issuing weapons without a form. He had been through this before and no one was going to tell him what to do. It was his armory. If anything was missing, there would be no one to pass the buck to, war or no war. He wasn't born yesterday.

A mob of soldiers milled by the armory window. Everyone was in a rush. The quartermaster asked each man for his serial number and wrote it down as best he could in the dark with a combination pen-flashlight. Then the pen ran out of ink, What kind of useless pens are these? he complained. Does anyone have another? No one did. He threw it down in disgust, shut the window, locked the armory, and went off to look for a new one. A reconnaissance officer drove up to ask for a pair of binoculars. "What are you standing there for?" he shouted when told the quartermaster was looking for a pen. "Are you out of your minds? Do you have any idea what's going on? Men are dying up there and you're looking for pens?" He kicked an ammunition crate as hard as he could. It burst open and dozens of greased Uzis scattered on the ground. Everyone grabbed one and ran to their tanks. Bundles of straps were lying on a table. Whoever could, took one.

"'Gunner!' Gidi shouted. 'We're moving out!' I grabbed an Uzi and ran to the tank. There was no time for a strap.

"I took the Uzi and a canteen of water, vaulted through the turret by pressing my elbows against the cockpit, and leaped from the tank. The ammunition could blow up at any moment. Eli was already on the ground, exhausted from loading shells all morning. He was haggard and sooty, his tanker's suit drenched in sweat. In one hand he held a grenade. Gidi was next to him.

"'Wait!' I yelled. 'Where's Roni?' He was still in the driver's compartment. Perhaps his earphones were dead. Bullets were flying all around us. 'Roni!' I screamed at the top of my voice. 'We're hit! Get out!'

"'I can't,' he answered quietly. 'I can't open the hatch. Your gun's blocking it.'"

"Every tanker knows that a gun blocking the hatch traps the driver. It's his only exit. That's why every driver warns his gunner to make sure the gun is off the hatch before bailing out. As we were crossing the Jordan, Roni had said to me 'Whatever happens, don't forget the hatch.'

"I climbed back into the tank, ran to the gunner's compartment, and tried working the swivel. The power traverse didn't respond. The alternator was dead. It never worked when you needed it. I tried the manual crank. It barely moved. I gave it a whack. We were sitting ducks. A disabled tank is a gunner's favorite target. Whoever hit us the first time would fire again, this time at the turret. They must have practiced the same things we did. The crank was turning now. I lowered the breech block to the turret and asked, 'Roni, can you get out?' 'No!' he shouted. 'Swivel it more to the right. Quick!' I heaved at the crank with all my strength. It didn't move. Something was stopping it. My hand ached. I picked up a kilo hammer that Eli had found in a driver's toolkit at Yiftach and swung it as hard as I could. Nothing else mattered in the whole world. The crank turned. It turned some more. I managed to open the right-hand hatch door and called, 'Roni! Can you get out?' 'Almost,' he said. 'A little more. I can almost get my head through.'

"I had no strength left to turn the crank. I hit it again with the hammer. And again. Roni pushed open both hatch doors. 'I'm coming out!' he yelled.

"I jumped quickly. Gidi pointed. 'That way. Run!' We ran doubled over across black rocks, under a hail of bullets. The Syrians saw us and opened up with machine guns. Ricochets bounced off the rocks. I kept low and zigzagged the way we were taught to do in basic training. Our instructor was a hardened paratroop lieutenant named Volberg. We were a mixed company of *yeshiva* students and *kibbutzniks*. 'Get this straight, you mongrels,' he had said. 'I'm going to teach you soldiering. I'm going to hammer it into your thick skulls.' Whoever didn't keep his head down had to carry a full stretcher up and down a hill in boot camp seven times in the middle of the night. 'You'll bitch about it now,' Volberg said. 'But you'll thank me in the next war.' Who was thinking of the next war?

"Eli collapsed on the ground. He was beat. All morning he had loaded shells without a break. 'I can't run any further,' he said. 'I've had it. You can go on without me. It's hopeless anyway.'

"'What's the matter with you, Eli?' Roni yelled. 'Run! We can't stay here.'

"'Come on,' I said. 'Run by my side.' A ricochet whistled above us. 'We're almost out of range. Just a little further. Come on, Eli.'

"He picked himself up. Gidi was running ahead of us. He didn't hear us calling to him to wait. After a while he turned around and pointed to his ears, crossing his hands back and forth. 'He can't hear,' I said to Roni. Although he didn't look wounded, there was no time to examine him. We kept running, crossed a road, and dived behind a dirt embankment concealed by eucalyptus trees. The Syrians were shooting at anything that moved. We saw Tiktin's tank back up and reach the road. Roni suggested filling our canteens from its jerry cans. They were almost empty. Who knew how long we would be stranded here? He stood on the embankment, took a few steps, flung himself down, and crawled quickly back to us. The Syrians had sprayed bullets at him. Gidi and Eli hugged the ground. Roni and I peered over the embankment. A shell set Tiktin's tank ablaze. Tiktin and another man jumped out of it. They were burning like torches. They rolled on the ground, dowsing themselves from a jerry can. They rolled all the way to the road. There was no way of reaching them.

"A white Ford Escort sped down the road from north to south. We jumped to our feet, desperate to flag it down. It was our only lifeline. Tiktin's too. Roni said, 'It's probably some journalist risking his neck for a story.' We waved at it, praying it would stop. We might not have another chance. But the driver didn't see us. He was going too fast. We kept praying. The car sped off. We watched it vanish. What now?"

Long afterward, I found out more about that car. It was a stroke of luck its driver hadn't seen us. Man's doings are of the Lord; how can a man then understand his own way?

A year after the war, our battalion held tank maneuvers. There, I came across Tiktin, commanding a tank. I stared at him. His face was scarred. I couldn't believe he was alive.

"How did you survive?" I asked him. "I saw you in flames."

He said: "We were on fire when we jumped from the tank. We put it out by rolling on the ground. My eyes were covered by blisters. I had to pry them open with my fingers. We crawled to the road. I saw a Ford Escort traveling fast. I knew it was our only hope. Somehow I managed to flag it down. I'll never know how the driver saw me. He saved our lives."

Who would have saved them if he had seen us first?

The three officers looked at me. I continued: "We lay behind the embankment, which had a view to the north. Roni saw tanks approaching. They were Syrian T-55s. You couldn't mistake them. One of our Skyhawks appeared overhead and began to attack them. We were in a bad place to be. I told Eli to get up, Roni pulled Gidi to his feet, and we moved on. We reached the Tapline road. There was a culvert beneath it. Gidi stopped to look at it. Someone suggested hiding in it. We had to talk to him in sign language. Gidi was against it. He didn't think we had put enough distance behind us.

"Gidi was not in good shape. Apart from his hearing, he was having trouble with his eyes. No one knew what was wrong with him. Roni took his hand and we started to run toward Wasit Junction. The ground beneath us was shaking from explosions. A Syrian APC passed close-by, firing in all directions. We ducked and avoided being seen. Then there was a boom and it burst into flames. Something roared above us. We looked up and saw jets. Roni thought they were Soviet Sukhois. They flew low, almost right over us. We ran some more until we came to a protected dip. Gidi stopped and we sat down. He took off his helmet and checked his ears. The only damage was a dent in his helmet where a bullet must have hit it. 'I can't hear,' he said quietly. 'I don't know why.' He stretched out on the ground. So did Eli. They were dead tired.

"Roni and I took turns standing guard. There were explosions all the time. Our situation wasn't good. We were four crew members with no tank, a deaf commander, two Uzis, one with and one without a strap, a percussion grenade, and a single half-full canteen. Our task force had been put out of action. We had seen it burn tank by tank. It was just a matter of time before the Syrians found us. We could hear their trucks on the Tapline road. We couldn't expect reinforcements. The entire brigade had been thrown into the battle. Our battalion was wiped out. The Syrians had taken Nafah.

"We had to think clearly, logically. I felt the pocket of my shirt. There was a small book of Psalms there. It was my mother's. She had given it to me when I left for the war. It had her tear stains in it. She always read it on Sabbath afternoons. *A psalm to David. The Lord is my shepherd, I shall not want. He makes me lie down in green pastures; He leads me beside the still waters. He restores my soul. He leads me in the paths of righteousness for His name's sake.* It was the Psalm my father sang before the *Kiddush* over wine after coming home from synagogue on Sabbath mornings. His melody was soothing. I had always associated it with the tranquility that graced the world on Sabbath mornings. But now another verse struck me. *Yea, though I walk through the valley of the shadow of death, I shall not fear, for Thou art with me.* It was as though David had written it just for me. What was it that made you feel that all his Psalms were about you, like a portrait whose eyes stayed focused on you from every angle?

"An airplane fell from the sky. Ours or theirs? The rumble of artillery kept up. Who was firing? At what? Where were the Syrians? Would they comb the area and find us? Would the mechanized infantry company be sent in now? Its men had been disappointed they were going to miss the war. Perhaps by now they were in it and would find us. We would have to signal them that we weren't

Syrians. We could use a pair of *tzizit* as a flag. And maybe the three tanks that had broken down before the bridge would turn up too. We had seen mechanics working on them on our way to the river. They might have been fixed.

"It was hard to think straight. We drank some water. First we said, 'Blessed art Thou O God, Lord of the Universe, by whose word all was made.' How much you could find even in a simple blessing over water!

"'We'll stay here until dark,' Gidi decided. 'Then we'll go back to our tank. It's safer at night. No one will notice us in all this chaos. I think all that was damaged was a tread and the sprocket drive. Maybe the turret was hit too. We can fix that. If Roni can give us some play with the clutch, we'll get the tread off. We'll pry it with a crowbar and a five-kilo hammer. We'll cut out the damaged part, rejoin the task force, and go on fighting on shortened treads. You don't abandon a tank.'

"No one knew what he was talking about. We didn't have a crowbar. We had no tools at all. How were we going to get to the tank? How were we going to fix it? There was no task force left to rejoin. You couldn't get a tread off without a spanner. And even if some of the attacking force had made it to Hushniya, we had no map, radio, or way of finding it. All we had was a deaf commander. Syrian tanks were still pouring down from the north. Sooner or later we'd be spotted."

No one spoke. Eli sat off to one side, gripping his grenade. Suddenly he blurted:

"I don't know about you, but I'm not going to be taken prisoner. If they come, I have a grenade."

We had all heard stories about what the Syrians did to our prisoners-of-war.

"Eli," Roni said quietly, as if he were disputing a *Talmudic* passage with a study partner, "how can you say that? You know it's forbidden. The Bible says: *He who sheds any man's blood shall have his blood shed.* The rabbis say 'any man's' means your own too."

The two of them turned to me.

"Of course it's forbidden," I said.

Eli parried by citing King Saul and the Philistines. The Book of Samuel said in plain language that Saul chose to take his own life rather than fall into the hands of his enemies. Eli had read that a commentator at the time of the Crusades cited this passage as permitting suicide if a man feared betraying his religion.

Roni and I were adamant. The law was clear. Suicide was strictly forbidden. King Saul had nothing to do with it.

Eli said:

"What will you do then? Fight the Syrians with two Uzis? Surrender? Be taken prisoner?"

Gidi tried following the argument by reading our lips. He wasn't able to. We fell silent. After a while Eli asked:

"What will be? Do you think the Syrians will take Tiberias? Who'll stop them, the divisional clerks?"

Leaving Camp Yiftach, we had seen rear-echelon troops sitting at the crossroads at Rosh Pina with their rifles. And maybe the Tiberians themselves would turn the tanks back with Molotov cocktails, as in the stories we had read as children about the War of Independence. If our engineers were able to blow up the Jordan bridge, that too might slow them down. How could we lose the war? The Redemption was under way. The State of Israel was proof of it. Could the Redemption be militarily defeated?

I told Eli: "I don't have an answer for you. But I do have a story."

Sometimes, when I'm out of answers, I think of stories.

This one was about World War ii. When Rommel was advancing through Egypt, and the Jews of the Land of Israel, fearing the worst, drew up plans for a last stand on Mount Carmel, Chief Rabbi Yitzhak Herzog of blessed memory predicted that no German army would ever reach them. After the war he was asked by someone who knew he never spoke rashly: what made him go out on such a limb. Had he had a vision? How could he have known what God was planning?

The chief rabbi answered that he was not a prophet or inspired, just a Jew with faith in the Sages. There was a saying of theirs, he said, that the Temple would not be destroyed a third time, nor the People of Israel driven again into exile. Unfortunately, whether because he had forgotten or for some other reason, he failed to reveal where this saying was to be found. The scholars were still looking for it.

Gidi watched us talk. He knew we were debating a religious point. He said, "I don't know what you're talking about or what your books say, but I do know one thing. We're going to win this war. We're going to win it because we have to."

No one answered. I remembered studying in the *yeshiva* that, although it was forbidden to make special vows in return for God's help, this ban was rescinded for those in distress. I tried thinking of what I might vow. In the end I made up my mind. The one thing I was sure of was that the world would never be the same.

"The minutes passed. Roni and I took turns standing guard. Gidi fell asleep. Roni suggested that we crawl forward to a better vantage point. We did and oriented ourselves by the fence along the Tapline road. The sun was low. The light was beginning to fade. We drank some more water. Gidi was feeling stronger. 'Let's head back to the tank,' he said. First we recited the afternoon prayer. We poured out our hearts until we were literally trembling. Then we said the 130th Psalm. In the yeshiva we used to say it for someone who was critically ill: *From the depths I called You, O Lord. Lord, hear my voice; let Your ears be attentive to the sound of my pleas…I put confidence in the Lord, my soul put confidence, and I hoped for His word. I yearn for my Lord, among those longing for the dawn, more than they that watch for the morning.*

"We started out for the tank, following Gidi. *For His anger endures but a moment; in His favor is life; weeping may endure for a night, but joy comes in the morning.* A truck passed on the road. We ducked. Ours or theirs? We walked doubled over, keeping parallel to the road. From the high ground looking down on a crossroads we spotted a half-track and some soldiers. Ours or theirs? It was impossible to tell. Roni spotted a hole in the Tapline fence. It looked like a good place to cross. What if it was mined, though? We talked it over and decided to risk it. Just then we saw a tank. This one was ours, for sure. We knew our own tanks and walked to it. A soldier was perched on the turret. We recognized him. It was Yossi. He hugged us with emotion. The rest of the crew was sitting on the tank too. They were as much in the dark as we were. They had been the lead tank out of Camp Yiftach on the first day and had taken a wrong turn and driven all the way to Ein Zivan without realizing the Syrians were at Nafah. When the brigade found out where they were, an infantry patrol was sent to retrieve them. Now they were waiting for orders. Yossi offered us something to eat, a few wafers and cans of sardines. Gidi was against wasting time. 'Every minute counts,' he said. 'We have to get back to the tank and go on fighting.'

"We headed on toward the quarry. Apart from the trucks passing on the road, the silence was eerie, palpable. A few hours ago the ground had shook with the sounds of war. Now the shooting had stopped. Nothing stirred in the twilight. Tanks lay scattered all around, charred and disabled, their guns pointing in all directions. Some were totally destroyed. One had lost its turret. Another lay on its belly. There was no one in sight. We made for our tank without bothering to reconnoiter. We could see it from a distance. It was right where we had left it.

"Nothing made any sense. What had happened here? Who had stopped the Syrians? Perhaps our covering fire had helped after all. Perhaps we had turned them back or slowed them down, or some of the attacking force had broken through to Hushniya. Where else could it be? And where were the crews of the burned tanks around us? The numbers on them were still visible, written in ink on white jute bags tied to their ammunition holds. 4. 2-A. 1. We walked to our tank. Gidi wanted to fix it and go on fighting. You didn't abandon a tank. You didn't quit in the middle of a war. We would catch up with the rest of the force. It must be on its way to Hushniya. Those were the brigade commander's orders the night before the battle at the quarry: 'You'll push on to the Hushniya pocket. Good luck!' That was last night. Now it seemed like last year.

"'We'll rejoin the battalion,' Gidi said. 'You don't abandon a tank. We have to keep fighting.'

"We neared the tank. We were practically at it when Gidi announced he could hear again. He took off his helmet and asked me to say something.

"'Gunner to commander, do you read me?' I said loudly, almost shouting.

"'Yes, gunner. I read you loud and clear.'

"Roni went to inspect the driver's compartment. It was full of shrapnel. The sprocket drive was badly damaged. Gidi and Roni checked the tread to see if it could be shortened. I climbed onto the turret and hold Number 9. We stowed all our personal equipment there. I undid the bands of the rear machine gun, removed the two heavy rings of the rolled-up camouflage net and pushed it aside, opened the hatch, removed the jerry can of water and opened several crates of machine gun rounds whose bullet belts were tangled in disorder, and came to my pack. It was crushed but intact. Quickly I opened it, fumbling with a stubborn buckle, and took out my prayer book and phylactery bag. The initials of my name were embroidered on the bag beside a Star-of-David in golden thread. My mother called the star a 'Zion.' That was the word for it in Egypt. I gave the bag a loving kiss."

It was on the day of my *Bar Mitzvah* that I donned those tefillin for the first time, in the early Morning Prayer group of the Maimonides Synagogue in the immigrant project of Beit Mazmil. The congregants were working men who prayed at sunrise in order to get to work on time. Many had welfare jobs planting trees in the forests around Jerusalem. The men of my family—my father, Uncle Nino, Uncle Jacques, and Hakham Binyamin—stood around me, showing me how to tighten the phylactery box on my upper arm, how to wind the leather thongs seven times to my wrist, make the letter Shin with them on the back of my hand, and finish with three rings around my finger while saying, *And I will betroth thee unto Me forever; yea, I will betroth thee unto Me in righteousness, and in judgment, and in lovingkindness, and in mercies. I will even betroth thee unto Me in faithfulness; and thou shall know the Lord.* A shiver ran down me. I bound the thongs to myself with such love and devotion that they almost stopped the flow of blood. Days later their marks were still on my flesh. The women in the women's section threw candies and cried "Mazal Tov! Mazal Tov!" and the old rabbi of the Maimonides Synagogue, Hakham Salman Hugi Abudi, came up to me. I thought he would congratulate me too. Yet placing his hand on my head, he opened a volume of Maimonides and read aloud:

"He who dons his *tefillin* regularly will live a long life, for it is written, *O Lord, by these things men live.*"

He continued to read the laws of *tefillin*, ritual fringes, and *mezuzahs*:

"Every man must take care with the *mezuzah*. Each time he enters and exits a door, he must think of God's unity, and remember His love and rouse himself from his slumber and torpor in the follies of Time, and know that nothing lasts except the knowledge of the Rock of the World, and then he will return to his senses and follow the straight path. Our ancient rabbis said: A man with *tefillin* on his head and arm, and ritual fringes on his shirt, and a *mezuzah* on his door is certain not to sin, since he has many guardian angels to warn him and rescue him, for it is written, *The angel of the Lord encamps round about them that fear him and delivers them.*"

When Hakham Hugi Abudi was finished reading, he said in a whisper that might have been either a blessing or a warning that I should not let a day of my life go by without putting on my *tefillin*.

It was sunset. For the first time since my *Bar Mitzvah*, a day of my life had almost passed without putting on my *tefillin*. I kissed them and slipped them onto my arm, feeling the same shiver of love that I had felt in the Maimonides Synagogue. I tightened their box on my arm without binding the thongs and hurriedly placed the second set on my head before it was too late.

Roni was on the tank, inspecting the treads. He saw me and said:

"What's wrong with you? Can't you see the sun has set? Don't you know you don't put on *tefillin* after sunset?"

I ignored him. I didn't believe the sun had set. There was still a red glow in the sky. I wasn't going to let the day pass without putting on my *tefillin*. I bound the thongs to my arm, praying that the sun was still hiding behind the mud huts and trees on the horizon. Yet even as I recited the "Hear O Israel" to testify to the oneness of God, doubt gnawed at me. If only the clouds would part and reveal the sun in all its splendor, as had happened to Nakdimon Ben-Gurion in the story we learned as schoolchildren.

Once, the story went, the People of Israel made the pilgrimage to Jerusalem and there was not enough water in the city to drink. And so the famous Sage, Nakdimon Ben-Gurion, went to the Roman procurator and said, "Let me have the use of twelve springs for the pilgrims and I will either return the water I have taken or pay a penalty of twelve talents of silver." The procurator agreed and a day was set for payment. Yet when it arrived, the winter rains had not yet fallen and there was no water in Jerusalem. In the morning the procurator sent a message to Nakdimon saying, "My water or my money!" "I have time," the answer came back. "The payment is not due until sunset." At noon Nakdimon received another message saying, "My water or my money!" Back again came the answer, "I have time." The afternoon passed and a third message said, "My water or my money!" And again Nakdimon Ben-Gurion replied, "I have time." The procurator mocked him and said, "Does he think the rain that has not fallen all year will fall now?" Then he went to the bathhouse.

While the procurator was taking his bath, Nakdimon Ben-Gurion went sadly to the Temple. He wrapped himself in his prayer shawl and said, "Lord of the Universe! You know that what I did was not for my own honor, nor for that of my family, but for Yours alone, that Your pilgrims might have water to drink." At once the sky darkened and the rain poured down until it gushed from every spring in Jerusalem. The procurator left the bathhouse as Nakdimon Ben-Gurion was leaving the Temple. Their paths crossed in the street and Nakdimon said, "You owe me for the extra water I returned to you." The procurator replied, "Although I know it was only for your sake that your God turned His world upside-down, I still have the right to my money, because it rained after sunset." And so Nakdimon Ben-Gurion returned to the Temple, wrapped himself in his prayer shawl again and said, "Lord of the Universe! Let Your love for Your favorites be known." At once a wind sprang up, scattering the clouds to reveal a last sliver of sun. When the two men met again the procurator said, "I have lost twelve talents of silver to a man who could make the sun rise in the West."

Such was the faith and love of the ancient rabbis and the miracles performed for them. I lifted my eyes to the sky, searching for a last ray of sunlight. Lord of the Universe! Let Your love for Your favorites be known.

Miracles don't happen every day.

The psychologist sitting across from me in the shack at Tel Hiros handed me some water and urged me to drink. I said the blessing and took a sip. The debriefer arranged his papers in front of him and attached a paper clip to a form. He marked the form with a red pen, measured it halfway across with a ruler, punched a hole in it, stuck it into a blue cardboard file holder, wrote something in red on the cardboard, and circled that in black.

I waited.

"We're listening," the psychologist said, looking at me. "We're listening to every word. Go on."

I went on.

"We sat by the tank, debating what to do. By now even Gidi understood that we couldn't fix it. It needed a repair shop, or at least a mechanic with a proper toolkit. Gidi suggested splitting up.

He and Roni would look for a mechanic, fix the tank, and rejoin the force while Eli and I found another tank that needed a gunner and a loader. We mustn't waste time. Every minute and every tank counted. We opened a tin of crackers that had been tied for who-knew-how-long to the front of the tank and had something to eat and drink.

"Eli went to look for a new helmet. The one he had didn't fit. It was tight, just like mine. He climbed into the driver's compartment of a disabled tank and jumped out a second later, looking horrified.

"Large birds hovered over us. Gidi said they were scavengers. They were common in this part of the Golan. We tried driving them away without success. From somewhere came the howls of jackals and the barking of dogs. We walked back from the quarry to the crossroads. On the way we passed a small camp. Roni said it had belonged to the UN. An old Sherman tank was parked nearby and several mechanics were working on it. 'They've even thrown in the Shermans,' Eli said. But we needed Centurion mechanics. In the camp we found a tent with some blankets. It seemed a good place to sleep. 'It's perfectly safe here,' Gidi said. 'Safer than Tel Aviv.' I went with Roni and Eli to forage for food and water. We headed for the army base at Nafah. A patrol of paratroopers came by on the road. 'You crazy tankers!' they yelled. 'Where do you think you're going?' Syrian commandos, they warned, were in the area. 'Get back to your tank,' they said. 'It's the safest place at night and you may as well guard it.'

"We returned to the tent and lay down on the cots. The guns boomed all night. It was dark when we awoke. Gidi spotted a water pipe with a faucet and went with Roni to wash. They had to bang open the rusty spigot with a rock. I was watching them from the tent when machine guns began to fire nervously at the sky. It was the Sherman, blasting away. We looked up and saw Syrian helicopters about to land at the crossroads. One of our jets was maneuvering above them. Eli said it was a Mirage. It did a back flip, trying to shoot the helicopters down. They were close enough to the ground to see the soldiers inside them. There were dozens of them, large men in camouflage uniforms and battle gear, their faces daubed with mud.

"There were four of us with two Uzis, one with a strap and one without.

"The Syrian soldiers jumped out of the helicopter with their weapons. Before there was time to think, an APC filled with our infantry drove up and laid down a fusillade. We took our Uzis and headed on without a word.

"We never talked about it afterwards.

"A truck pulled up beside us. Its front windshield was smashed to smithereens. An officer asked if we were a crew looking for a tank. He would take us to a divisional rendezvous near Rosh Pina. Crews were needed for the tanks coming out of the repair shop. We climbed onto the truck. Gidi and Roni sat by the driver and Eli and I sat in back. Wounded soldiers were lying there. Someone on the road saw Roni and shouted, 'Roni, how badly were you hit?'"

Later we heard that the story had circulated that Roni was wounded and evacuated by truck. It even reached the yeshiva. His friends looked for him in all the hospitals. His fiancée heard the news too. And all that time he'd been with us.

I continued:

"We crossed the Jordan, this time back to Rosh Pina. The truck stopped and we got out to look for the rendezvous. What we saw was a strange sight: a crowd of soldiers was sitting in groups with its packs, eating chocolate chip cookies and drinking soda pop. We couldn't believe our eyes. Who were these men? Why weren't they up above? It wasn't clear if they were combat troops. We had thought every able-bodied man was already fighting. We must have looked as strange to them with our Uzis and filthy tankers suits as they did to us. We wanted to shout: 'Don't you know? There's a terrible war up there! We're coming from it. Every soldier counts. Every minute.' But we didn't."

We caught sight of Bentsi, the loader of 1-A. Red-eyed and grimy, he was wearing a NATO greatcoat with a torn lining that flapped in the wind. On his shoulder was an Uzi with back-to-back clips. "Listen," he said. "We have to find tanks and go back up. Men are dying. The Syrians are knocking out our tanks. They're still advancing. We have to stop them with our bare hands if necessary. There's no one else to do it. We need commanders, drivers, gunners. We have to get the tanks back into action. Long live the People of Israel!"

We followed him to some men who were waiting for tanks to come out of the repair shop.

"What happened to your tank?" I asked Bentsi.

He answered, the words tumbling out:

"We were in the battle of the quarry. All the tanks around us were hit. On one side of us a turret was lying by itself. On the other a tank had rammed its gun into the ground. Everything smelled of burning. We kept firing at the ridge above us. The driver of a tank next to us was leaning his head against the hatch of his compartment. 'Go see what's the matter with him,' my commander said. I recognized him right away. He had been killed on the spot. Maybe you knew him, the driver of 1-A."

We knew about 1-A. Bentsi went on:

"We kept shooting. The terraces were so steep that the shell conveyors kept falling off their rails. I had to scoop them up with one hand and the shells with the other while the tank lurched at crazy angles. The turret bucket was spinning. I kept falling too. I would get to my feet, fire a few bursts from the machine gun, load another shell, and fall again. There was such a smell of gunpowder that you couldn't breathe. You couldn't stick your head out for air, either.

"There was no time for the morning prayer that day. Between one shell and the next I said what I knew by heart plus verses from Psalms. I kept falling and getting up and lifting conveyors and loading shells and firing the machine gun while the tank filled with smoke. I had never prayed so fast in my life. Or so hard, not even on *Yom Kippur*."

He was reminded of something.

"Do you know where I was this *Yom Kippur*? In a new settlement in the Jordan Valley. The day before the fast someone drove up to our *yeshiva* in a van and said he's from a place called Argaman and needs men to make ten for a prayer group. It's our responsibility as Jews, he says. Several of us climbed into the van. The afternoon of *Yom Kippur* the army phoned the settlement with news that war had broken out. There were positions on the Jordanian border that had to be manned. Several men put down their prayer books and left. We went on praying, not knowing what to do. No one knew what was happening. When the fast was over we headed back for Jerusalem without eating. That's when we realized that the war was for real. I took a bus home to Kfar Ha-Ro'eh, which was also my unit's assembly point. First I went to see my parents. I must have seemed in a good mood because my father said, 'Bentsi, why are you laughing? Do you think war is a laughing matter?' He was a boy during the First World War, he lived through the Second, and he fought in the War of Independence and the Sinai Campaign. Now he had three sons in the army.

"An hour ago," Bentsi told us with emotion, "I saw my old headmaster, Rabbi Neriyah. He had driven up to the Golan to encourage the soldiers. He thought the fighting was further north and that he was coming to a rear base—and suddenly he was on a battlefield. No one realized how far the Syrians had reached. He was evacuated here and I ran into him. He showed me a charred prayer book he had found in a *tefillin* bag in a burned tank at Nafah. I didn't tell him what I'd been through. I didn't want him telling my father what a hero he has. My father has a bad heart. I asked the rabbi to tell him he had seen me here, far from the front. That's all he needs to know."

He continued:

"We were on the road to Sindiana. Toward evening we engaged eight enemy tanks and knocked them out. We were moving again when the battalion commander shouted over the radio, "There's a missile heading straight at you!" Our driver backed up and it missed. "You're yellow!" the battalion commander laughed. We headed on for Sindiana. The plan was to join a column led by Danon. He was facing a big Syrian force and kept radioing us to hurry. He was on his own and needed help.

"Our tank stalled. We had run out of fuel and didn't know what to do. It was getting dark and the place was crawling with Syrians. Just then we saw a tank coming toward us. It was Hanan's. It had no radio and had to be signaled by hand. We thought we'd transfer our equipment to it. But mortar shells were falling all around and we ended up running for it like crazy. I grabbed my tank helmet and this Uzi with the clips. Guess who Hanan's driver was: Elhanan, my old *yeshiva* buddy from Kfar Ha-Ro'eh! But there was no time to talk. Our crew sat on the sprocket wings. Nothing was working in Hanan's tank. The power was out too, but at least the tank could move. He was taking it below for repairs. A tank with no traverse or radio wasn't going to help Danon.

"The terrain was rough. Elhanan could hardly see. Rami, the platoon second, sat on the front wing to direct him. We were given a ride as far as the helicopter pad near Alika. There was a stand of eucalyptus trees there. We got off in the dark and walked toward it. It was very cold. Two French journalists were sitting in a car. They let us warm ourselves in it while they stood outside in the cold. I put on my *tefillin* without a blessing, because it was already night. We heard shouts and incoming shells. Everyone dived into a ditch by the road. I ran for it, tripped over a wire, fell, hurt myself, got up, and ran some more. Then I tripped over a rock and fell again. After a while a fuel and ammunition convoy came by, heading south toward the Customs House. I hitched a ride with it. The shells were still falling. By the time it occurred to me that fuel and ammunition weren't the best company in an artillery bombardment, it was too late to change my mind. Anything could have blown us sky-high. I rode as far the Customs House. I got off there, lay down by an old wall, and fell asleep.

"In the morning I was awoken. 'Tanker!' a divisional quartermaster was shouting at me. 'What are you doing here? Why aren't you with your tank?'

"'It's disabled,' I said.

"'I'll bet,' he said to the sergeant next to him. 'First they abandon their tanks and then they come back down and say they're disabled.'

93

"I could have slugged him. I was too furious to say a thing. I bit my tongue, clenched my fist, and kept quiet. A car heading back toward Nafah gave me a lift. Levi, the brigade second, was in it. He was organizing a new force. Tanks were coming out of the repair shop and needed crews. It was he who brought me here. Come on, let's find a tank and go back up."

He was almost shouting. The torn lining of his coat flapped in the wind. Long live the People of Israel!

I told the three officers:

"A group of tankers was waiting beneath a eucalyptus tree. Each was sitting by himself. Whenever a tank was ready, an adjutant came to ask for a crew to man it. I was a gunner. I waited for a tank that needed one."

I talked without stopping for breath, in a single long sentence. None of the officers interrupted me. I suppose I didn't give them a chance to. I felt strange when I finished, as if I had given away a part of my soul. I was sweating and shivering. And I was seeing things again. I had thought I was over that and now it was back. I wasn't the only one. Years after the war I was told by Elhanan that passing anywhere near Nafah quarry still gave him the shakes.

The three officers in the shack waited for me to say more. The debriefer looked up questioningly from his papers.

"You wanted to hear about one day of the war?" I said, rising. "Well, you've heard."

For a while they just stared at me. Then the debriefer turned back to his papers and checked something off. The psychologist stood up, put one hand on my shoulder, and gave me a long handshake with the other. He didn't say anything. When I turned to leave, he motioned to me to sit down again. I supposed he wanted me to listen to the next story. Maybe he thought it would do me good to hear that others had had the same experiences.

The fact was that, although we had served in the same battalion, fought in the same places, and been together afterwards, I knew nothing about what anyone had gone through in those first days of the war. I didn't know if they were at Nafah quarry, or whether they had pushed on to Sindiana, or been in the breakthrough at Khan Arnaba, or left Yiftach with adjusted sights or a radio that worked. For some reason, I had never wanted to ask. Nor had anyone asked me. Now I would listen to Elhanan. I sat on the bench.

He would talk about the battle at Nafah. Perhaps, I thought, I would find out what had happened to Dov.

Chapter nine

The officers called Elhanan. Hanan left the shack. He had commanded Elhanan's tank and knew his story. Perhaps he didn't want to hear it. Perhaps he had other things to do.

Elhanan walked to the table with measured steps. His dark blue eyes had a dreamy look. He took a seat and faced the officers. After a while he spoke in a deep, soft voice. He talked slowly, almost in a whisper, pausing after every few words to think about what came next. Sometimes his voice trembled.

"We were the lead tank of our platoon," Elhanan said. "Hanan was the commander. Shammai was the loader. Nachman was the gunner and I was the driver. Nachman was supposed to be married in two weeks. 'This is a war of survival,' I told him. 'The law is that everyone has to fight, even newlyweds exempted by the *Torah*.' He knew that as well as I did. But his heart wasn't in it.

"We left Camp Yiftach with another tank on the afternoon of the first day. Its commander was Rami, the deputy platoon leader. We were a column of two tanks."

I had heard about those two tanks. On a visit to our battalion,

Levi, the brigade second, had told us about the first two tanks to reach Nafah on the first day of the war. "They saved the Golan," he said.

Sasha thought Levi was talking about Hanan and Rami's tanks. Zada thought one of the tanks was Tsvika's. Itzik said they both were wrong because Levi was referring to Menashe and Yo'av. Who was to say? Perhaps they had all saved the Golan together.

Elhanan said:

"It was hard to say goodbye to my wife Malka on that night after *Yom Kippur*. I could see how worried she was. I too had a bad feeling. While we were packing my things, I talked to her about faith and trust in God's Providence. I quoted some verses from the Bible and from the rabbis. I knew that Providence is for the Jewish People as a whole and not for any individual. Even Jacob, though he was promised that God would always be with him, was frightened when Esau marched against him with four hundred men. But I managed to calm Malka down. We were still packing when Yoel dropped by to say goodbye and surprised me by saying that the verse *the Lord will not cast off His people, neither will He forsake His inheritance* doesn't apply to any single one of us, so that we all have to pray for our own lives to be spared. Either he had read my thoughts or we were all thinking the same thing. I hoped Malka didn't hear him. I don't think she did. Or else she pretended that she didn't. We put Daniel to bed. He lay there smiling at me. I kissed him, trying not to cry. Malka came with me to the assembly point. She stood watching the bus pull out."

Elhanan paused. The officers stared at the table. He said:

"We reached Camp Yiftach late at night. At once we started to run around, looking for equipment and ammunition. We were stacking shells when Nachman told me he was getting married. He was down in the hull with Hanan. 'What will be?' he kept asking. 'What will be?' I tried to reassure him. In a platoon of young reservists like ours, there was more than one soldier about to get married and more than one with a new wife at home.

"We left Yiftach a little before eleven in the morning. On the downhill road to the Jordan my gears jammed in neutral. I hit the shift with a hammer, the way we were taught on maneuvers, but it didn't help. I couldn't get the tank into gear. We were off to a war with no transmission. I braked so suddenly that the tank skidded off the road, knocking down a few trees and losing a bazooka mount. But at least that threw it into gear. We reached the army base at Nafah at about one o'clock and drove right into a battle. Syrian tanks were there. No one could believe it. Syrians at Nafah!

"We stopped by the gate of the base to decide what to do. There were infantry running in all directions while the Syrians shot at them. A half-track caught fire near the gate. Men jumped out and dived for cover. We heard the commander of the 188th Brigade giving orders over the radio. It was bedlam. We didn't know who to obey. On maneuvers there was always a clear chain of command: your platoon, your company, your battalion. Now no one knew what was happening. Syrian tanks were everywhere. The commander of the 188th was shouting, 'All hands! Retake the base!' All hands meant us. We had to push back the Syrians. I started to drive through the gate—and the gears jammed again. We were caught in a battle, everyone was shooting, and we couldn't move. Finally I shifted into first. Then the engine stalled. Hanan shouted over the intercom, 'Jump-start it in reverse!' It worked. We rolled backward and the engine turned over. I put it in forward gear and we drove through the gate."

Elhanan's story reminded me of something. The summer before the war, while we were on battalion maneuvers in the Negev, our tanks had kept stalling one after another. Someone asked what would happen in a real war. There was laughter. Who believed in real wars in those days?

"Did you enter Camp Nafah through the East or South Gate?" the historian wanted to know.

Elhanan's reply was a hand gesture that meant, "How should I know? Do you think we had a compass?"

The historian wrote something on the form in front of him and slipped it into the blue file holder.

I tried recalling whether there was an East Gate at Nafah. It must be important, I thought. Elhanan continued:

"Most of our infantry had been driven out of the base. No one knew from where we could launch a counter-attack. We drove up an incline and spotted five Syrian tanks. Nachman fired at two of them and hit both. They burst into flames. A shell exploded in front of us, kicking up a cloud of dust. A Syrian tank was facing us point-blank. Its next round was sure to hit us."

The debriefer asked: "Were you firing squash heads or armor piercers?" Elhanan thought about that. "You'll have to ask the gunner or the loader. I think they were squash heads." He went on:

"I heard Hanan shout, 'Driver! Reverse! Quick!' The gear engaged and we backed down off the incline. A second later a shell landed where we had been. It suddenly registered on me that this was a real war.

"The commander of the 188th was back on the radio. 'Charge the camp!' he was shouting. 'We've got them surrounded!' I didn't know what he was talking about. We didn't dare drive back up the incline. A dozen Syrian tanks were waiting for us. I glanced at my watch. It was three o'clock. I couldn't believe we had been fighting for two hours. Now Rami was radioing from the other tank. He needed help. He was stalled inside the camp, between the perimeter fence and some trees. He needed cables. We tried to spot him but couldn't. The trees were hiding him. He tried guiding us over the radio. We still couldn't make him out.

"Hanan saw a Syrian tank taking aim at us. Nachman fired at it. So did some other tanks. It began to burn. Black smoke billowed from it. You couldn't see a thing. You couldn't tell who was shooting at who or hitting what. We could have been bushwhacked at any time by a Syrian tank hiding in the trees. We changed position. It was crazy. There were tanks everywhere. You couldn't tell which were disabled and which weren't. Every minute someone shouted over the intercom that some tank that was out of action had us in its sights.

There was no knowing who might shoot at you. It was sheer chaos. I knew I had to keep calm.

"In the end Rami spotted us. He jumped from his tank and ran to ours. Shammai switched places with him, Hanan became the loader, and Rami took command of our tank.

"The radio kept ordering us to retake Camp Nafah. We hadn't moved far from the gate. A German shepherd was tied to it. She had a puppy and was going berserk from all the noise. She kept trying to free herself and couldn't. She looked at us, begging to be untied. It was heartbreaking. We were just as helpless as she was."

Elhanan paused to collect his thoughts. He didn't drink the water placed in front of him. He said:

"More men were pulling back from the camp. It was awful to see our army in retreat. I saw a squad led by an officer charge back inside, straight into the Syrians' fire. They crossed the road on the run, crouching low. A few minutes went by. Then they ran out again and re-crossed the road under heavy fire. The officer waited for the last man to cross before following. I thought: At least something is being done by the book. A soldier by a shelled-out building in the trees was talking into a radio while looking through a pair of binoculars. He must have been a forward spotter. I had no idea who he was spotting for, but I remember thinking he must be very brave."

"An air force reconnaissance officer or an artillery spotter?" asked the debriefer.

Elhanan didn't know. Through his periscope he had seen a soldier talking into a radio. That was all he could say.

The officer took a form from the blue file holder and jotted something down. The identity of the spotter must be important, I thought. I tried to remember if I had seen an air force reconnaissance officer. Perhaps if we had had a reconnaissance officer of our own, we wouldn't have walked into that ambush in Nafah quarry.

Elhanan used the interruption to order his thoughts again. After a few melancholy moments of silence he went on:

"The tank next to us was hit and set on fire. Hanan didn't want to look at it. Its commander was a friend. They had been in a course together. The driver came running toward us. He was in a state of shock. A half-track appeared out of nowhere, picked him up, and drove off.

"Another wounded man was heading for our tank. He was soaked in blood. He reached the turret and nearly passed out. Hanan bandaged him. He needed another field dressing and I gave him mine. The bandaged man came around quickly. Most of the blood, it seemed, wasn't his. Another tank pulled up beside us. There was no one in its turret. The commander was driving and the loader was guiding him because the driver had been hit. 'Do you have an extra driver?' the commander shouted. 'Me,' the wounded man said and moved to the other tank."

Elhanan broke off and put his head in his hands. He said:

"Later, I met that driver in an intensive commanders' course. Everyone with tank experience had been called up to it. His name was Peretz and he filled me in on what had happened to him. His tank had been hit in the quarry. He and two other men bailed out and ran to Camp Nafah, only to realize the Syrians had taken it. They ran some more. One was killed by a Syrian bullet. Peretz was wounded trying to retrieve him. It was the dead man's blood that was on him. The third man was too exhausted to keep running. He ducked into the camp commander's office, locked the door, and hid. He stayed there until we retook the camp. He even managed to phone home. He just picked up the receiver and dialed. The Syrians never found him. Afterwards, Peretz said, he was no longer right in the head."

Elhanan was given another glass of water. He didn't drink this one either. He shut his eyes and said hoarsely:

"We kept fighting until it was dark. Each time we spotted an enemy tank we fired, came down from our position, and went back up to a new one. When night came we drove down below to regroup. We were in Camp Sufa with ten other tanks. Morale was low. It was looking bad. The men lay tired and depressed on the sprocket wings. We broke out some rations. Rami was too worried to eat. 'What will happen tomorrow?' he asked Hanan. 'Who's going to stop them?' 'Another day like this,' Hanan said, 'and they'll take the whole Golan.' Nachman said there would be nothing between them and the Jordan, or even Tiberias. I was standing by the tank, saying the evening prayer softly: *For we are His people Israel ...He has ransomed us from the hands of kings...He has given our souls life and did not allow our foot to falter. He has guided us to the pinnacles of our enemies and raised us above our despisers...For the Lord has ransomed Jacob and redeemed him from those stronger than him...Lay us down in peace, O Lord our God, and raise us up to a new and good life, and spread over us Thy tabernacle of peace, and aid us with good counsel from before Thee, and save us speedily for the sake of Thy name, and protect us and keep from us all foes, pestilence, hunger, war, and grief, and guard our coming and our going that we may live in peace evermore, for Thou art the Lord who guards us and saves us...*

"It was the regular evening prayer. We say it every night. But that night it sounded different. Hanan and Rami heard me and came closer. When I was finished we began to talk. We talked about prayer and faith. I told them what we had learned in the *yeshiva* about faith in God and His promise to Israel. I mentioned how the prophet Samuel told us to be strong 'for the sake of our people and the cities of our God,' and of how the State of Israel is the first ray of the Redemption. The Sages compared the Redemption to the morning star: as the morning star shines alone in the blackness of the night until a bright sun lights the world, so the Redemption begins in darkness that will vanish. No one can predict the future. But we are promised that the destiny of Israel will not betray it and that God does nothing He repents of, for He is not a human being who repents. I said, 'The people of Israel will triumph even if there is no telling what will happen to any one of us.' Hanan and Rami stood listening. I don't know if I convinced them intellectually. I wasn't trying to. I was speaking from the heart to encourage them. To encourage myself too. Hanan looked at me and said, 'I hope you're right.' After the war he said to me, 'I envied you then for your belief. It must have made things easier for you.' 'I'm not so sure,' I told him.

"On the morning of the second day, we moved out at sunrise. We took the route to Nafah from Alika, skirting Camp Yitzhak."

"On the northern road?" the historian asked.

"Yes," Elhanan said. "We passed to the north of the camp. It was incredibly quiet. We were driving over yesterday's battlefield. All was still. It was a fine, clear day. The sunrise was glorious. It glinted off the houses of Nafah. I thought of the words of the Morning Prayer, 'May Thou light a new light over Zion and may we speedily see its glow,' and of how the Gaon of Vilna did not allow his disciples to recite those words. He said that God should be praised for the light that already shines, not for the light that will shine some day.

"We were a column of three tanks under Danon's command. I remember thinking, 'At last we're getting organized. The army is its old self again.' The chaos of the first day had gotten me down. It was a free-for-all. There was no communication. Each tank fought its own private war. Traveling in formation with proper radio contact cheered me up. Now we'll fight the way we've been taught to, I thought. But it only lasted a few minutes. Then the first tank broke down. We tried helping it. Other tanks joining up with other forces blundered into our column. The radio was too noisy to hear anything. It was full of static and different voices and commands, all meant for different people. The sun was in my eyes. I couldn't see the road ahead of us. All I saw was a curtain of white light. Rami guided me from the turret. We were told to move north of the quarry."

I was listening from the bench. Now, hearing Elhanan mention the quarry, I sat up. He was talking about the morning we had fought there. Those were the tanks that had passed to the north of us. I had spotted them in the periscope. A chill ran down my spine. I hadn't known whose tanks they were. The sun had blinded me. Gidi had wanted me to fire at them, although he was blinded too. I said I wasn't going to unless I was sure they were an enemy force. I had never found out if they were. Now I knew.

Elhanan continued: "Nachman and I were in our compartments. We couldn't see. I suppose that was a small mercy. Hanan and Rami had their heads out the turret and saw everything. Hanan's voice shook as he described it over the intercom. It was a horrible sight. Our burned tanks and half-tracks were all over the quarry. Every minute we were told of some new tank with its turret blown off or its gun shattered by a shell. Hanan tried reading the numbers on them. We came to a crossroads. An officer directed us toward some low hills to the south. We climbed to the top of one. It was covered with tall grasses almost as tall as a man. Rami tried radioing our force. At first it didn't answer. Then the reception was too poor to understand. Other voices drowned it out. We didn't know whose they were. From somewhere came the sounds of a battle. There were firing orders and someone shouted, 'We've been hit!' You couldn't tell who was fighting or shooting at what. That's when I realized that this war wasn't going to be won by tanks. It would be won by people, men like Hanan and Rami and Peretz.

"On maneuvers we had always moved in formation, in platoons, companies, and battalions, with regular radio contact. Now everyone was on his own. Whoever held out the longest would win. The realization hit me all at once. I just didn't know how long the longest had to be."

From the bench, I glanced at the psychologist. I was curious to see if he would write or say anything. He didn't. He just went on listening. Elhanan said:

"Rami was our commander. He decided to proceed without hearing from Danon. We headed east, on a straight line from the quarry to Mount Yosifon."

"You're sure it was east?" the historian asked. "From the quarry to Mount Yosifon?"

"Yes," Elhanan answered firmly. "I know it was east because the sun was still in my eyes. I kept looking for some landmark to steer by. In the end we found the rest of the force. There were other vehicles with it. I'm not sure who they belonged to. Probably a reconaissance unit."

"Your own brigade's?" asked the debriefer, opening his blue file holder.

Elhanan spread his arms wide to say, how should I know? He said:

"There was incoming artillery. At first we shifted position each time a shell landed near us. But after a while we saw that the shells were so dispersed that it was pointless. Rami decided to ignore them. Then someone shouted, 'Rockets!' Hanan ducked and something flew over him, trailing a wire that snagged on him. It took a lot of tugging and yanking to set him free. We didn't know it was a Sagger. The wire guided it."

"You knew nothing about Saggers?" the debriefer asked.

"No."

The debriefer murmured to the historian and wrote something down. Elhanan continued:

"We were told to change course for Sindiana. A Syrian force had turned up there. They kept coming back for more. We advanced despite the bombardment. Our orders were to engage them. First we had to find them, though. Nachman couldn't spot them through the periscope. We were at a tactical disadvantage. The land was flat and rolling gently toward us. The radio kept reporting Syrians in the vicinity. We moved slowly to keep from being surprised. No enemy was visible. All at once a geyser of dust flew up in front of us, followed by a boom. 'Quick, back up!' Rami shouted. 'The next round will get us.' The gear jammed again. Perfect timing! I used all my strength and wrestled it into reverse. We backed and changed position. A shell landed near us. The Syrians were concealed. Each time we moved, the dust gave us away. The tank next to us was hit and on fire.

"For me, those were the worst moments of the war. I didn't know what we had got into. I didn't know how we were going to get out of it. Any tank of ours that moved was hit. But we had to stop them. It was now or never. I thought: we've always been told to give our all—now we'll find out how much that is. We could do it. We had to.

"There was no time to think. We changed position again. Now we could see them. Other tanks followed suit. The radio reported Syrian tanks being hit. The tide began to turn. Hanan shouted over the intercom that some were retreating. Two trucks, most likely ammunition carriers, turned tail and ran. Our own tank had two sure kills to its credit. At last things were going our way, thank God. We kept firing. Nachman told us it was turning into a killing field. Now it was the Syrians who gave themselves away by moving. Enemy tanks were pulling back from behind the trees. As soon as they did, dust marked their position. Tanks, ammunition trucks, and other vehicles were in flames. After the war we learned that we had turned back the last Syrian attack on Nafah.

"The battle was hardly over when we received an order to' push on to Hushniya. We were told to follow Danon on a dirt track code-named Catacomb that linked up with the Mount Yosifon road. Rami reported that we were in a column of ten tanks, a serious force. Danon traveled quickly. We couldn't keep up with him. The gears kept jamming. The engine stalled each time I shifted into fourth. In the end I stuck to third, which was slower but surer. The tank ahead of us was commanded by Haggai, the CO of L Company. Danon kept radioing us to hurry. 'Where are you?' he asked. 'I've engaged a big Syrian force. I'm fighting by myself. Get a move on!' 'We'll be there soon,' we promised. 'We're coming.' It was no time to explain that our gears kept jamming or that we couldn't shift into fourth. There was another tank between us and Haggai. We were following it in a wadi when we saw a bright flash of light from Haggai's tank. We couldn't tell if it had been hit or was firing. The column halted. Rami called over the radio, 'Haggai, Haggai, over! Come in, Haggai! Haggai, Haggai, come in!' There was no answer. He kept calling. The tension mounted.

"Finally, we were radioed by the tank ahead of us. The left side of Haggai's turret had been hit. They would try to reach him. Meanwhile, Hanan spotted a Syrian anti-tank emplacement blocking the wadi. It was dug in well and hard to target, and there was no way to get past it. We backed up and looked for a detour. Danon was on the radio again. 'What's keeping you? Hurry! I'm fighting on my own.' 'Syrian tanks!' Nachman shouted over the intercom. We spotted three of them to the east of the wadi, where a gully ran off to the south. Hanan gave the order to fire. Nachman fired. So did the tank in front of us. All three Syrian tanks were destroyed. We were still stuck behind Haggai, though. The emplacement blocked our advance and we saw no alternate route. I suggested taking another crew member, some grenades, and a machine gun with a tripod and working our way to the emplacement's rear. I'd trained for that kind of thing in the infantry. We'd take it out and our column could advance.

"To me it seemed logical. But Rami wouldn't give me the go-ahead and meanwhile Danon kept radioing, 'Where are you?' I suggested it again. Rami still wouldn't agree. I felt rebuffed. What did he know about infantry tactics? But he insisted it wouldn't work and I had to drop it. He was the commander. Maybe he was afraid to be left without a crew. He had another idea. There was a point where the wadi looped closest to Sindiana at which we might be able to cross to the other side without being seen by the emplacement. Although the terrain was difficult, he decided to try it. We set out followed by the other tanks, heading east toward the gulley and crossing the wadi near the Sindiana woods. The channel was wider there. Halfway across it, shells started landing. There must have been more Syrian guns we didn't know about. Rami had to stick his head from the tank to guide me. Machine gun bullets flew around him. We could hear them bouncing off the armor. But he had no choice. The shells kept falling.

"We couldn't tell if they came from tanks or emplacements. We couldn't even tell what direction they were coming from. I had the gas pedal pressed to the floor. 'What's holding you up?' Danon radioed. We jounced over rocks and terraces. It was like driving down the stairs of a tall building. The bullets didn't stop bouncing off us until we were behind the southern rim of the gully.

"We'd made it. My lips murmured the line from the evening prayer, *'He has given our souls life and put not a snare before our feet.'* But we'd paid a price for it. Our radio was out, and so, Nachman reported, was the power swivel. All our electrical systems were down. Without them, the tank was useless. We must have damaged the collector. Rami ordered me to halt. There was no point in linking up with Danon. He didn't need a tank without a radio or gun swivel.

"It was four in the afternoon. There was nothing to do but head back for the repair shop in Alika. I had killed the engine. It wouldn't start again. Luckily, we were on a slope. I jump-started it and didn't switch it off a second time.

"On the way to Alika, we saw a tank crew running toward us. One of them was Bentsi. It was good to see a familiar face. We must have seemed to them like angels from heaven. Their tank was stuck, it was getting dark, and they were stranded in a place crawling with Syrians. But their radio was working and Rami got through to Danon and requested permission to continue to the repair shop. Danon insisted that we join him no matter what. Rami explained our situation again. In the end Danon agreed that we would be of no use to him. Our tank had to be repaired.

"We had no radio. Rami guided me. He sat on the wing with the safety off his Uzi and gave me directions. Syrian soldiers might be hiding behind any terrace. We passed the tanks we had knocked out earlier. One was a bridge-layer. Its bridge had been blasted in two. It had been on its way to the Jordan. If we hadn't stopped them, they might have crossed and pushed on to Tiberias.

"There were steel hulks as far as you could see, trunks, jeeps, tanks, T-54s and 55s. Hanan stopped by each Syrian tank to check for enemy soldiers. There was nothing but corpses in them. He had a shocked look. God Almighty, what a world of killing and grief!"

Elhanan's words made me think of a legend in the Midrash. "When the Holy One Blessed-Be-He created Adam," it went, "He took him and showed him all the trees of the Garden of Eden and said, 'See how fine and beautiful are my creations. All are for you. Take care not to ruin or destroy My world, for if you do there is no one to repair it.'"

Elhanan continued: "We drove on and came to some disabled tanks of our own. Hanan and Rami went to look for wounded tankers. They didn't find any. They came back in silence, looking stunned. We had been fighting for two days, but now their faces had something new in them. The light had gone out of Hanan's eyes.

"We reached Alika in the evening. That was the end of Day

Two. Each day was so long. It was a blessing we didn't have to fight at night. Neither we nor the Syrians were equipped for it. Hanan went to bring an electrician from the repair shop. We were dead on our feet and starving. But we also needed fuel, water, and light and heavy ammunition. Rami went to get them. They didn't come all at once. First one truck came, then another. That gave us no time to rest.

"The big ammunition truck arrived last. We began transferring the shells. It wasn't the first time we had had to load an empty tank with shells, but we were exhausted and the ammo crates were old. It was a struggle to remove each shell from its casing. I was too bleary-eyed to lift them. The crates fell on me until I was black-and-blue. I kept cutting myself with the screwdriver with which I had to force the metal catches. My hands were full of blood.

"It was after midnight. Someone came to tell us that a tank force was being organized at Camp Yitzhak. We drove there. Hanan went to find the commander and ask what his plans were. I opened some cans and tried eating. Don't ask me what I ate. I wouldn't have known the difference between canned meat, corn niblets, and grapefruit sections. I just shoveled it into my mouth. Two spoonfuls were all I got down.

"We were woken before dawn on the third day. It wasn't four o'clock yet. The force was ready to move in half an hour. We drove in a blacked-out column without taillights, behind a reconnaissance jeep. The terrain was unfamiliar. I was nervous and stayed as close as I could to the tank ahead of me. Danon was the commander again. We didn't know who was in the other tanks. After the war I heard that Shlomo was there, and Itzik, and some others from the *yeshiva* and the battalion.

"How did Danon get to Camp Yitzhak?" the debriefer wanted to know.

"I have no idea," Elhanan said. "You have to remember that the fighting in those first days was in a very concentrated area. Every night we went back below to regroup."

He went on: "It was the morning of the third day. It was

slow going. But our mood was better. At least we were moving in an organized formation.

"The column kept halting. In the end we took up positions in Sindiana. The plan was to ambush a Syrian force that was expected to counter-attack toward Nafah. The first light was dawning in the east. We were dug in on two hills with enough trees and old ruins for concealment. Danon was on our right. Two other tanks were in forward observation posts. The visibility was poor. There was morning fog and the sun was in our eyes. Even standing in the turret, Hanan couldn't see. Rami tried changing position, but that didn't help either. The radio reported enemy forces advancing toward us but still far-off. This time the odds were in our favor. We were ready for them. We would let them walk into our trap. Our tanks were hidden and had surprise on their side. The only problem was the sun.

"The Syrian force was about three kilometers away. Clouds of dust marked its route. The radio said it had reached Ein-Warda. Our orders were to hold our fire until it came within effective range. Voices on the radio were discussing its size and composition.

"Suddenly, Danon opened fire without warning. We knew right away that something had gone wrong. Later we were told that another column of ours had spotted the Syrians from Tel Shifon and opened fire. When they scrambled for defensive positions, Danon joined in. We should have started firing too, but we couldn't see anything to aim at. Danon reported knocking out a tank. Only when the Syrians began shooting back did we make them out by the flashes of their guns. Now we had targets. Nachman fired at one of them, missed, made a correction, fired again, and scored a direct hit.

"Shells were falling near us. We were in a pitched battle again. My lips were murmuring more verses. The tank closest to us pulled back, its gun disabled. We changed position in a hurry. The radio reported heavy Syrian losses. Then the return fire stopped. The last Syrian tanks stopped moving.

"It was quiet. But not for long. Reports came of more enemy tanks. Soon they were firing again. We had thought we had seen the last of them, but there were many more of them than we had counted on. Nachman fired at the flashes. The shells were landing close again. We changed position. We had lost the element of surprise. And the sun was against us. We were staring straight into it."

I too had prayed that day for the sun to go behind a cloud, if only for a second. Elhanan said:

"Rami shouted, 'Driver, reverse!' I was sure we'd been hit. But it was just a shell falling very close. *Who gives life to our souls and puts not a snare before our feet.* Rami had a shrapnel wound in the cheek. He could barely speak. A tank near us burst into flames. A rescue team ran to pick up the wounded. Then our power swivel went on the blink. Without it we couldn't shoot. Hanan bandaged Rami, took his place in the turret, and radioed Danon that we were disabled. Reports of more wounded came in over the radio. Getting to them was hazardous. It meant crossing exposed ground. Danon ordered Hanan to retrieve as many of them as he could and return to the repair shop in Alika. He was going to fight on, even though he was left with only one other tank. What strength that man had! What courage! I remember wondering, who would ever know about people like him and what they did?

"We began picking up wounded. Hanan would find a protected fold of ground, tell me to stop, jump from the turret, and run to get someone. One man was badly hit in the stomach and legs. Hanan carried him on his shoulder and hoisted him onto the turret. There was no room for him in the hull. He lay on the tank without a sound. Hanan was too exhausted to talk. Nachman moved to another tank to make room and we headed back down to Alika at full speed. Two tanks passed us, going the other way. We didn't know where they were coming from or heading for. We told them to reinforce Danon, who needed all the help he could get.

"We reached Alika and began unloading the wounded. Suddenly we were surrounded by a group of French-speaking photographers taking pictures of us from every angle. One of them all but climbed onto a wounded man to snap him. No one knew who they were or what they wanted. Some elderly reservists helped us to lower the wounded from the tank. They looked at us as though we were heroes. I didn't tell them there was nothing heroic about a tank whose gears jammed every time the shooting started. Hanan ran to get the mechanics. Tanks were waiting in line ahead of us, but he managed to wangle a place at the front. He also found a loader and a gunner. They were from the 188th Brigade that had been chewed up on the first day, holding the Syrians in the southern Golan. They still looked in shock. We didn't ask them about it. We refueled the tank and stacked fresh ammunition and replaced the coaxial machine gun, which had been put out of commission by shrapnel.

"Hanan went to tell Levi, the brigade second, that we were rejoining Danon. Levi was standing by a jeep. He and Hanan were talking when he received a radio message. He signaled us to wait and listened with no trace of emotion. When he signed off he said to Hanan quietly, 'You'll stay here. Syrian commandos have just landed from a helicopter near Nafah Junction. I have no one to defend this base with. You know I've sent Danon every last tank that can move. Yours is the only one I have left. I need you here.'

"The radios blared in every vehicle. Word of the commandos spread. Everyone knew they were in the area. One man even claimed to have seen them jumping from the helicopters. He said they were advancing on Nafah."

I sat listening to the story of the commandos who had landed at Nafah Junction on the morning of the third day. I had to restrain myself from jumping to my feet. I wanted to say, "Yes, right! Right! I saw them too. It was at Nafah Junction and they were mowed down immediately." But I let Elhanan go on. He said:

"The staff soldiers around us were stressed. Who was going to protect them? The brigade second stayed calm. He leaned against the jeep and gave orders. We stayed in the tank. There was a roar of jets overhead. Someone said they were Syrian MiG's flying cover for the helicopters. There was a dogfight. We heard booms. An airplane fell. A parachute opened. A pilot dangled between the sky and the earth, his life hanging by a thread. We prayed for him without knowing if he was ours or theirs. Another MiG circled over the hills. We were all jumpy. The Syrians were still on the move.

"In the end, the commando force was wiped out. The brigade second told Hanan to join Danon. We made tracks for Sindiana with another tank. Things were still touch-and-go there. Danon had received reinforcements, but the Syrian counter-attack was at its height. His tank was firing non-stop. Just as we took up a position, the tank next to us was hit. It was a deputy platoon leader's. He bailed out and came aboard our tank. Our loader went to his tank, Hanan replaced the loader, and he became our commander.

"We received an order to advance. The Syrians were falling back. Their fire had dwindled. Some of their tanks were in full retreat. We took the offensive, swinging out in a flanking arc to the west. Although we met no resistance, it was getting dark and the road was littered with large rocks. The radio ordered us to attack Ramtaniya. You couldn't exactly call what we were doing attacking, though. It was more like running an obstacle course. Then we began to take incoming artillery. We didn't know where it was from or who had spotted us. Tank shells were falling too. We were in another battle. Leave it to our tank to stall again! I jump-started it. Everyone was shooting. Danon shouted over the radio, 'Spread out! Keep moving! Fire at anything that shoots!' The platoon deputy couldn't see anything that was shooting. Most likely we were too far in the rear. Danon kept shouting.

"The terrain was difficult. Bullets whizzed around us. It was getting too dark to see. Danon gave the order to cease fire and head back. The darkness had kept us from pressing our advantage. That was too bad. We had been on the verge of breaking the Syrians' lines. Now they were firing again. We managed to disengage.

"That night we regrouped. Another day of the war was over. The third."

Elhanan fell silent. He still hadn't reached the breakthrough at Khan Arnaba or to the battles of Kafr Nassaj and Halis. I knew he had plenty to say about them too. But we had each been asked to talk about one day.

Yom Kippur fell on a Sabbath that year. The brigade moved up to the Golan on Saturday night and fought until the middle of *Sukkot*, the Feast of Tabernacles. The first four days were a holding action. The push into the Syrian bulge started on Thursday, the first day of *Sukkot*.

I had described Days One and Two. Elhanan had gone on to Two and Three. Now Shlomo would talk about Five and Six. The first days of the war had seen him waiting by the Jordan bridge. Now he would tell about the breakthrough and the battle with Iraqi tanks at Khan Arnaba.

Elhanan rose. The officers opened their blue file holders and wrote. Elhanan joined me on the bench. He took out a small volume of the *Mishnah* from his pocket and began to read.

I had listened to his whole story and hadn't found out the most important thing. I still knew nothing about Dov.

Chapter ten

I t was Shlomo's turn. He wore a white crocheted skullcap, the work of his young wife. She had made it for their wedding a month before the war. The white ritual fringes of his *tzizit* stuck neatly out of his pants. He had the usual sparkle in his eyes and his good smile. He wanted to tell the three officers about the breakthrough at Khan Arnaba. He had fought as a gunner in Vagman's tank, the battalion commander.

I had heard about the Iraqi tank column that Shlomo was the first to engage, as it advanced toward our brigade's bivouac. He had knocked out seven tanks single-handedly before anyone could get organized. Now I would hear the whole story. It came punctuated with verses from the prayer book and the Bible, as though they were an intrinsic part of it.

"Since this is the first time I'm telling anyone about these things," said Shlomo, "I'd like to begin by thanking the Lord for watching over me, for it is written, *O Lord open my lips and my mouth may tell Thy praise.* With your permission, I'll read a few verses from Psalms."

He took a small Psalter bound in plastic from his shirt pocket, where it was kept with his field dressing and POW card. He opened it and read slowly, stressing each word as if in prayer:

> *O God, why has Thou cast us off forever? Why doth Thy wrath smolder against the sheep of Thy pasture?*
>
> *Remember Thy congregation, which Thou hast purchased of old; the rod of Thine inheritance; which Thou hast redeemed; this mount Zion, wherein Thou hast dwelt.*
>
> *Lift up Thy feet unto the perpetual desolations; even all that the enemy has done wickedly in the sanctuary.*
>
> *Thine enemies roar in the midst of Thy congregations; they set up their ensigns for signs.*
>
> *A man was famous according as he had lifted up axes upon the thick trees.*
>
> *But now they break down the carved work thereof at once with axes and hammers.*
>
> *They have cast fire into Thy sanctuary, they have defiled by casting down the dwelling place of Thy name to the ground.*
>
> *They said in their hearts, Let us destroy them together: they have burned up all the synagogues of God in the land.*
>
> *We see not our signs: there is no more any prophet: neither is there among us any that knows for how long.*
>
> *O God, how long shall the adversary reproach? Shall the enemy blaspheme Thy name for ever?*
>
> *Why withdrawest Thou Thy hand, even Thy right hand? Pluck it out of Thy bosom.*
>
> *For God is my King of old, working salvation in the midst of the earth.*

Shlomo closed the Psalter and replaced it in his shirt pocket. He said:

"We no longer have Prophets to explain what Heaven is telling us. *Neither is there among us any that know how long.* But I'm certain we're being spoken to and that it's up to us to understand. King David says: *Thy enemies roar in the midst of Thy holy times. They have burned all the synagogues of God in the land.* The war broke out on *Yom Kippur*, the holiest day of the year, and on the first day of *Sukkot* we broke through the Syrian lines. On *Yom Kippur* we fought to pleas for mercy and on *Sukkot* to psalms of thanksgiving. When we sat in our *sukkah* in Alika before the final push, I prayed: *And spread over us Thy tabernacle of peace.* And when we blessed the Four Species, I thought of the words of the Sages, 'Because Israel observes the commandment: *And yet shalt you take upon the first day the fruit of the citron tree,* it is victorious over Esau, who is meant by the word 'first,' for it is written of him, *And the first was born red all over.*'"

Shlomo paused and launched into his tale.

"The final push began at Alika on the first night of *Sukkot.* Every tank in the brigade that could travel on its treads, and every crewmember who could still stand on his feet after the battle of Nafah quarry, was there. My own crew wasn't at the battle of Nafah. Our tank broke down before we could get there. But when we reached the quarry on the evening of the second day, we saw what had happened.

"That night at Alika, crews of mechanics worked around the clock to get every tank into fighting condition. The crews refueled and stacked ammunition. Adir built a *sukkah* over a hole made by a mortar shell and asked me to inspect it. It met all the requirements: it had walls over twelve handbreadths high, and enough room for a small table and the bulk of a man, and an awning of eucalyptus branches that kept out more sun than it let in. It was permitted to recite the blessing over wine in it and the blessing 'Who has commanded us to sit in a sukkah,' and to eat a holiday meal in God's presence. The Sages said that the commandment to dwell in a tabernacle on the feast is like the commandment to live in the Land of Israel, for it is written, *In Salem also is His tabernacle and His dwelling place in Zion.* In both the tabernacle and Zion we are surrounded by holiness. In both we are commanded to live our ordinary lives—eating, drinking, sleeping, and so on—in the midst of holiness. And just as living ordinarily in the *sukkah* is the commandment's fulfillment, provided we do nothing improper, so it is in the Land of Israel: the mere act of dwelling and walking and planting and earning a livelihood there is performing a divine task. There was even a Sage who said, 'The commandment demands your whole body, even your shoes and boots.'

"I went to bring a bottle of wine that we had been keeping in the tank.

"In Nafah, on the evening of the second day, there was an army chaplain handing out Bibles and books of Psalms. I took a Bible and some bottles of *Kiddush* wine. One broke on the way to Khan Arnaba. We used the others for the blessing over wine on the Sabbaths and feast days of the war.

"Many tank crews came to our *sukkah* to say the blessing. Each had its own story. After reciting the *Kiddush*, I hummed a *Hasidic* tune of my father's that we had sung at home around the table—'*And thou shall be glad in that feasting...*'

"Those were words of the *Torah*, but it was hard to be glad far from home. Here I was, alone. '*When a man has taken a new wife, he shall not go out to war, but he shall be free at home one year, and shall gladden his wife, which he has taken.*' And yet here I was alone. We had married a month earlier.

"The day before had been a hard one. We had fought in the battle of Ramtaniya that Elhanan told you about. There was heavy bazooka fire. Tanks were hit. We kept shooting. At one point a shell landed right next to a tank in front of us. The tank backed up without noticing we were behind it and ran into us. Our radio went dead on the spot. 'Move her up!' Vagman yelled to the tank's commander. When it was free of us, we discovered that we had also lost our power steering. Vagman decided to advance in a straight line. Then we heard him firing his Uzi from the turret. A Syrian infantry soldier was trying to climb onto the tank with two hand grenades. You had to hand it to him: it took guts. I was in the gunner's compartment and couldn't see what was happening. I only know he almost made it to the turret. Then Vagman said quietly, 'I killed him.'

"We couldn't fight without power steering. We were told to

pick up as many wounded as we could and return to the repair shop in Alika. Vagman ran and brought back five wounded men under fire. Two were in total shock. We gave them first aid and water and headed for Alika. On our way we dropped some of the wounded off at a first-aid station in Nafah. That was where I saw my first dead covered with blankets. The wounded lay groaning on stretchers. I hadn't realized how bad it was until then. It hit me hard. But good things had happened on the day before *Sukkot*, too. A few minutes before the holiday began, I noticed an open door, entered an office, and found a telephone. Without thinking, I picked up the receiver. An operator answered. 'Can I have a line?' I asked. 'Why not?' he said. 'One minute.' It was mind-boggling to be able to phone home like that in the middle of a terrible war. I dialed, and my wife answered. We had only been married a month. I was too choked-up to talk. 'Happy holiday!' was all I could say. 'I'm okay. Happy holiday!'

"We brought two squares of army biscuits in place of *challah* to our *sukkah* and ate the holiday meal. Then everyone hurried back to the tanks. I asked Vagman for permission to sleep in the *sukkah*. I had always done that on the holiday. Vagman wasn't religious and had no idea what it was about, but he agreed. I blanked out and fell asleep at once. Two hours later he woke me and told me to get back to the tank. There was a Syrian artillery bombardment. We had to be at our stations.

"On the morning of the fifth day, the first day of the feast, there was time to pray and bless the Four Species. I had brought an *etrog*, a citron, from home. I always buy one in advance to keep the commandment to start preparing for the Feast of Tabernacles right after *Yom Kippur*. The smallest commandment makes a difference. The Sages said, 'A man should always consider both himself and the entire world half-sinful and half-just, so that even a single commandment can tilt the balance.' And the citron, the only one of the Four Species to both smell and taste good, stands for the man who has both knowledge and good deeds.

"Amichai brought a willow branch, some myrtle leaves, and a palm shoot, and we blessed them, shaking the palm shoot in all directions to keep the evil winds away. The smallest details of a commandment can prevent misfortune. I pictured us in an ark on angry waters and I prayed: 'Hosanna! Save us! Save us for Your sake, O Lord! For Your sake, our Redeemer, save us! Save this, Your people, and bless Your inheritance and safeguard them and carry them in Your arms forever!'

"At eleven o'clock Vagman assembled us and said, 'We're moving out to the jumping-off point.' We headed for Mount Avital in four columns, all the remaining tanks of our brigade. Our column was commanded by Sassi and had eleven tanks. Vagman was the second-in-command. Ahead of us, our artillery was softening up the enemy's positions. Our jets were attacking too. At last we were taking the offensive. At two P.M. the order came to move on Kuneitra. We were assigned to the covering force and took positions overlooking the advance. We could see the first tanks breaking through. They belonged to the division's Second Brigade. Many were hit, mostly by anti-tank weapons. We laid down covering fire. Tanks were burning. My brother-in-law was a gunner in the Second Brigade.

"Later that afternoon, the covering force was ordered to advance too. Over the radio we heard that Amos, the commander of one of the columns, had been wounded. Uri, our battalion CO, kept up radio contact with us. He had a calm, reassuring manner. Then, all of a sudden, he went silent. After a while we received a message he'd been hit. We were worried. He had led us into battle from the first day. We didn't know what had happened to him.

"A few more minutes passed. Then we heard Uri's voice again. 'I'm back,' he said. 'I was in the command half-track. Now I've switched to a tank.' He didn't have to say any more. We understood that the half-track had been hit and that Uri had managed to escape.

"Sassi was out in front, moving fast. He had a new, diesel-powered Centurion. Our own tank was an older model that ran on gas. We couldn't keep up with him. He kept radioing us to catch up. We were holding up the rest of the column. 'Where are you?' Sassi shouted. 'I need help.' But our steering was acting up again.

Then our driver lost control while accelerating and plunged into a trough, ramming our gun into the ground and plugging the muzzle with stones and earth. At the last second I managed to clear my legs, keeping them from getting caught in the turret bucket. That's the nightmare of every tank gunner. *He has given our souls life and put not a snare before our feet.* We managed to extricate ourselves. By then the rest of the column had passed us. Now we were at the end of it. We didn't know if a gun full of stones could be fired. There wasn't much time to think about it. We came under Syrian fire and Vagman ordered me to shoot. I was on target—the only problem was that the top third of the gun barrel flew away with the shell. We were left with a sawed-off shotgun. Even though we kept firing, we couldn't hit a thing. The turret filled with gunpowder fumes. We switched to the machine guns, advancing all the way to Khan Arnaba with a cannon that didn't shoot. Luckily, we were mostly facing missiles and bazookas, because there weren't many Syrian tanks left. But they could do plenty of damage too.

"That night we took up positions. It was the end of the first day of the feast. The sky was lit by an orange glow. There were fires everywhere. Every couple of minutes we heard the boom of a tank exploding with its ammunition. We couldn't tell whose it was. In the distance we saw concentrations of Syrian infantry in jeeps and trucks. We fired our machine guns at them. But our tank had reached the end of the line. Crews from the other tanks came to strip us for spare parts. We gladly gave away what we had. Soon we would head back for Alika. I was finished with the war.

"Just then a tank pulled up alongside us. Its commander told Vagman he couldn't go on and asked to be replaced. Vagman didn't think twice about it and switched to the other tank. I was feeling sorry that he wouldn't be coming with us when the tank's gunner climbed aboard our tank. He wanted to know who our gunner was. Everyone pointed at me. The man said his back was hurting him and that he was returning to Alika too. I looked at him. 'Your back?' I asked. 'Yes,' he said. 'It hurts.' 'It hurts?' I said. 'Yes,' he said. 'I can't go on. You'll have to take my place.'

"Vagman was already on the turret, transferring his equipment. He lifted his pack and said to me with a look that expressed everything, 'Shlomo! You know what I think.' He didn't have to say more. I took my bottles of wine and my *tefillin* and switched tanks. The two of them went back to Alika.

"*This is the Lord's doing, it is marvelous in our eyes.* Who knows what those Iraqi tanks might have done if Vagman and I had gone back instead?

"The next morning we were ordered to head south and widen the bulge. Sassi led the column again. We passed several villages. Anti-tank weapons were fired at us from each of them. Sassi's tank fired back at a wall and a ricochet hit him in the head. We stopped to give him first aid. Vagman took over the command. Now we were at the column's head. Vagman's face was black with soot. His hair was long, he was unshaven, and he was our new CO.

"Around noon we came to a village called Nasaj. There, Vagman decided to take a break. Abandoned Syrian fuel tankers and ammo trucks were parked there. We got out of our tanks. It was our first chance since early morning to relax. Some of the men took off their shirts and washed themselves with water from the jerry cans. Others opened rations on the sprocket wings. The drivers checked their engines and we all stretched out to get some sun and breathe some air that wasn't full of soot and gunpowder. Peace and quiet at last! As far as we knew, no Syrian tanks were ahead of us. We could smell the end of the war.

"All our tanks had their radios on, tuned to the battalion frequency. Since Vagman was now the CO, our tank monitored the brigade network too. Someone was listening at all times. Suddenly the division radioed: 'Rest time is over! Everyone back to your tanks! There's a large force approaching you.'

"We were taken by surprise. Vagman reacted at once. Without waiting for an order from the brigade commander, he took our crew and headed out. No one else was organized. We climbed a hill. Through the periscope I spotted dozens of tanks moving toward us in a single file. I said to Vagman, 'Do you see what I see?' 'Yes,' he said quietly. 'Should I open fire?' I asked. The lead tank was already in my sights. 'Wait,' he said.

"The sun was in their eyes. They couldn't see. They were heading straight toward us without suspecting anything. I doubt if they even knew where they were. The closer they got, the itchier I became. What was Vagman waiting for? It was better to fire before we were spotted. They came closer. My finger tightened on the trigger. I still had the lead tank in my sights. 'Not yet,' Vagman said.

"They were at close range when he ordered, 'Shlomo, fire!'

"I couldn't afford to miss. I was one gunner facing a column of tanks. I fired. 'Direct hit!' I shouted. 'Fire again,' Vagman said quietly. I fired again at the same trajectory. Another hit. 'Fire again,' Vagman said. I kept it up. We knocked out seven tanks. By then the rest of the force had arrived and was knocking out more. Vagman came down to the gunner's compartment and hugged me. He had tears in his eyes. Yossi, who had been loading one shell after another, asked anxiously, 'Shlomo, how'd we do? Any hits?' Uri, the brigade commander, radioed his congratulations. 'You did it,' he told Vagman. 'You can lead the whole brigade tomorrow.' Some prize, I thought. Then our jets arrived and spent the rest of the day mopping up.

"It was only later that we found out we had been facing an Iraqi expeditionary force. An entire fresh brigade. God knows what it was doing there or what made it want to start up with us.

"The sun began to set. It was a Friday afternoon. I said the Sabbath eve service in my tank, '*Leha Dodi*... Come, my love, to meet the bride,' and '*Mizmor Shir Leyom HaShabbat*... A hymn to the Sabbath day,' and the other prayers. I had so much to thank God for. I poured out everything that had been in my heart since *Yom Kippur*.

> *For all thy destroyers shall be destroyed,*
> *And all thy devourers shall be devoured.*
> *And over thee then shall the Lord,*
> *Rejoice like a bridegroom over his bride.*

"Then we headed north in a pitch-black night. We led the brigade. I spotted friendly tanks and informed Vagman. He halted the column. We joined up with the friendlies and bivouacked for the night.

"I took out a bottle of wine and made *Kiddush*. '*Who has sanctified us with His commandments, took pleasure in us, and with love and favor given us His holy Sabbath, as a heritage, a remembrance of Creation. For that day is the first of all holy convocations, in memory of the Exodus from Egypt For Thou hast chosen us and sanctified us above all nations...*'"

The three of us rose to leave the shack. A new trio, Sasha, Zada, and Tzion, was waiting outside for its turn. I already knew their stories.

I had learned many new things from Elhanan and Shlomo. One mystery, though, was still unsolved.

I walked back to the tank, thinking about it. I remembered my mother asking with a piercing look, "What happened to Dov?"

"I don't know," I had answered. "On maneuvers we were always together. He was the loader and I was the gunner. But this time the crews were mixed up. Everyone jumped on the first tank to come along. Every crew grabbed whoever it could; there was no system to anything."

Footsteps sounded behind me. I turned around and saw one of the officers. He was calling me.

"There's something I wanted to tell you," he said. "After your tank was hit, you mentioned finding your *tefillin* bag with its embroidered Star of David. That reminded me of another such bag that I heard about from a Golani Brigade soldier named Momo, or Shlomo. He found it in the loader's compartment of a burned tank at the foot of Mount Yosifon. The tank was totaled. The bag had a name embroidered on it. I thought you might want to know."

He turned and walked back to the shack.

I shouted after him, "What was the soldier's name?"

The officer raised his arms skyward in a gesture that meant, "Don't expect me to remember that too."

Chapter eleven

We returned to our daily routine, counting the days until the next leave. Each day was like all the others. The nights were long and cold. The only excitement was when Kimmel the adjutant arrived. We all ran to him. First, he attended to battalion matters. Then he untied the packets of mail and chatted with Hanan while we waited impatiently to see if we had received any. It was our only link with the outside world. Someone read aloud the names on the envelopes while Zada and Pasha made cynical jokes.

I was in the tent one day when Tzion called me. Kimmel had come with the mail. I ran to the shack. My name was read several times. There were some army postcards and a few letters, mostly from schoolchildren. Before the war I had taught a twice-weekly sixth-grade class and now my pupils wrote me once a week. I didn't know if the idea was theirs or their principal's. I could tell which letters came from them by the childish handwriting on the envelopes, and I put these aside while glancing at my other mail. There was a letter from a soldier I knew named Yair. He had never written me before and I couldn't imagine why he was doing it now. I tore open the envelope and read:

"Greetings to all lovers of God's *Torah*! I hope you are well. I've heard that your unit had a tough time of it. With God's help, the dawn will yet break. We learn this from the Book of Genesis, in which it says: *And Jacob was left alone, and there wrestled a man with him until the breaking of the day. And when he saw that he prevailed not against him, he touched the hollow of his thigh.* And the passage ends: *And the sun rose upon him.* Now Jacob was named *Ya'akov* because this means 'Heel-holder,' for we read: *And the first came out red all over like a hairy garment, and they called his name Esau. And after that came out his twin brother, and his hand took hold of Esau's heel, and his name was called Jacob.* Although he was not the first to emerge, Jacob refused to give up and continued the struggle. Nor will the struggle between him and Esau end until the break of dawn, for it is written: *For thou hast wrestled with God and with man and hast prevailed.*

"You must be wondering why I am writing to you. I was a study partner of Dov's in my *yeshiva*. He spoke about you a great deal. I thought you might want to know something.

"You probably know that I'm in the artillery, not in the tank corps like you. I finished my regular army service a few months before the war and hadn't been assigned yet to a reserve unit when it broke out. On its second day I was sent to Rosh Pina with a group of similar cases. No one knew what to do with us. We were sent from base to base, and each time a different commander had to decide what to do with us. We were told we would form a new unit as soon as guns were available, but meanwhile there weren't any. Eventually we were sent to Sinai and took part in the crossing of the Canal. That's a long story that I haven't the strength to write about now. What I wanted to tell you was something else.

"On Tuesday, the fourth day of the war, we were back in Rosh Pina, running from storeroom to storeroom to scrounge equipment. Suddenly we were told that gun carriages had arrived at the far end of the base. We ran to get them. Next to me was a boy from my *yeshiva*. He said to me, 'You know, they found his *tefillin*.' 'Whose?'

I asked. 'Dov's,' he said. 'Your study partner's.' That came as a blow, even though in those days you heard bad news all the time. I said, 'Dov? They found his *tefillin*?' He said, 'I heard his tank was found burned at the foot of Mount Yosifon. It was hit on the afternoon of the first day. No one knows what happened to the crew. A phylactery bag was found in the loader's compartment. There was a name embroidered on it.'

"That's all I know, except that I also heard that two of the crew members managed to escape. Maybe they can tell you what happened to him. And maybe you know more than I do. After all, you were up on the Golan. But someone told me you're still trying to find out. I thought you'd want to know. The two of you were such good friends."

Chapter twelve

On the Sabbath day, a Jew is expected to eat three festive meals. Whoever does so, the Sages said, will be saved from three misfortunes: the birth pangs of the time of the coming of the Messiah, the wars of Gog and Magog, and the punishments of Hell. There are those who eat a fourth meal, too, immediately after *Havdalah*, with its blessings separating the Sabbath from the rest of the week. They set the table even if they are not hungry and serve a dish they have not yet eaten that day, and gather round, still in their Sabbath best, to bid the Sabbath Queen farewell. Such, said the Sages, is the practice of beloveds who are about to part. Following the grand banquets given by each in honor of the other, they say, "Now let us dine together, just the two of us, for the hour of separation is near."

The People of Israel have a beloved whose name is the Sabbath. All the other days of the week have their mates: the first day has the second, the third has the fourth, and the fifth has the sixth. The Sabbath alone has none. And so the Creator said to it, "You are alone and Israel is alone—let Israel be your mate."

As though she were their bride, the People of Israel welcome the Sabbath each week by making themselves new, and choosing the finest wines for the bridal feast, and singing odes of praise and speaking words of wisdom at it, and doing still more pleasant things. And when it is time for their beloved to depart, they detain her with a last, private meal to keep the memory of her alive during the drab week to come. They sometimes call this meal the Feast of David, for it is like the fourth leg of a chair whose other first three legs are named for Abraham, Isaac, and Jacob.

The Sages of old held that every man possesses a small bone in his body that is nourished by this Fourth Meal and from which he will be resurrected on Judgment Day. This bone does not decay in the grave, for it drew no sustenance from the fruit of the Tree of Knowledge with which the serpent seduced Eve and contaminated her with its pollution. And why is this so? Because Adam and Eve ate the forbidden fruit on the Sabbath eve of the week of Creation, while the small bone is nourished from the Fourth Meal alone. Whoever partakes of the farewell meal for the Sabbath Queen is thus amply rewarded.

The People of Israel love the Sabbath and do all they can to enhance it. We, who had been up on the Golan for months, loved it even more. November came and went. It was now December and our homes were still our tanks, in which we had lived since *Yom Kippur.* No one knew when we would be going home. Many had left young brides there. Not only were they kept from performing the commandment that says, *When a man has taken a new wife, he shall be free at home one year, and shall gladden his wife which he has taken,* they were not granted even a month. Others had wives who were pregnant, or little children who missed them, or businesses that were in trouble, or studies that had been broken off. Even those who sought to keep their studies up had to manage without books or the ability to concentrate amid a thousand distractions. And that was apart from the memories of the horrors we had been through and the friends who were killed, not to mention the freezing cold, and tanks flooded with rainwater that needed constant attention, and the mud everywhere. The sky was low and gray. A piercing wind blew all the time.

All week long we waited for the Sabbath. When it came, whoever was not on patrol or standing watch joined in friendship and joy. Each one of us dressed specially for the occasion. Some had white skullcaps that they wore only on the Sabbath. Others laundered their tanker's overalls the day before. I myself was lucky to find one day, in a package of fresh clothing received from the quartermaster, a brand-new army belt of the kind ordinarily worn with dress uniforms. I kept it and used it only on the Sabbath. It made me feel as elegant as if I were wearing a fancy suit and tie.

Our Sabbath meals were special too. Not that they didn't consist of the same rations that we ate every morning, afternoon, and evening for months on end: sardines, and tinned mackerel, and canned meat, and canned stew, and corn niblets, and peas, and lima beans, and grapefruit sections. But on the Sabbath we added the chocolate bars, soft drinks, and other things that we bought and saved from the PX truck that came around during the week.

There was one of us who never failed to come back from his twenty-four hour leave without a can of *gefilte* fish. "This is for the Sabbath," he would say and it fed twenty men. Each of them tasted in it all the tastes he had dreamed of tasting that week. Word of our *gefilte* fish spread through the battalion. Soldiers, officers, tank crews, infantry patrols, medics, radio operators, city boys, kibbutzniks—all came for a taste of the Sabbath and there was always enough for more. I can't say whether this was a miracle or merely a result of our self-restraint. I only know that no one who came for our *gefilte* fish ever went away disappointed.

Even our conversation was different on the Sabbath. Not that we didn't talk about ordinary things too, but we avoided upsetting or worrisome ones and never mentioned tanks or war or missing home or the friends we never would see again. Although not all our words were words of *Torah*, none breached the peace of the day. During the week, whoever remembered anything unusual from his studies would make a mental note to relate it on the Sabbath. Whenever anyone received an interesting letter from his *yeshiva* he'd think to himself, "I'll read this aloud on the Sabbath." Anything illuminating, encouraging, edifying, or uplifting, from the uncommonly sublime to the sublimely common, was saved for the Sabbath.

On Sabbath eve we would wait for the sun to sink low and we would gather between two tanks. Our oil-and-grease-stained hands were clean. The worry was gone from our faces, replaced by a Sabbath glow. We sat on empty ammunition crates and sang the hymn we had sung to welcome in the Sabbath in our *yeshivas*:

> *Dear Friend of my soul, be Thou merciful,*
> *Bend Thy faithful servant to perform Thy will.*
> *May Thy loving friendship always sweeter be*
> *Than the sweetest nectar and all honeyed tastes.*

This hymn was composed in the seventeenth century by Rabbi Elazar Azkari of Safed, whose soul pined away for its Creator. In his *Book Of The Devout* he wrote, "*It is the way of the desirer to praise the Desired One in song and my soul sings to God in its desire for Him.*"

We shut our eyes and let the melody well up in us, thinking of the better days before the war. Each of us remembered welcoming the Sabbath in his *yeshiva*, an open book before him. I pictured the Western Wall in Jerusalem, where my fellow students and I greeted the Sabbath Queen. I saw the fine Jews of the city arrayed in their many prayer groups: groups of *Hasidim* in their gabardines and fur *shtreimels*, groups of *Mitnaggedim* in their long coats and broad-brimmed hats, groups of *Sephardim* in their white skullcaps embroidered with gold, groups of tourists in their brightly colored yarmulkas, all pining for the Sabbath and calling: "Come, O Bride, O Come, O Bride!" And she, the Sabbath bride, would come slowly, slowly, yielding to their entreaties while the doves fluttered their white wings like bridesmaids carrying the train of a bridal gown. Now the hymn graced the air of the Golan.

O Exalted One, Beacon of the world,
My soul grows faint with yearning and with love for Thee.
My Lord, I beseech Thee, cure its ailment now
And reveal to it the bliss of Thy radiance.
Then will it be succored and regain its strength,
Always and forever Thy true bond maiden.

Ancient One of old, let Thy mercy stir,
And show Thy compassion to Thy loving son.
Many are the days now that my soul has pined
To behold the grandeur of Thy majesty.
My God, I implore Thee, Most Precious of my heart,
Hasten to me, hearken, and ignore me not.

Reveal Thyself, my Dear, and spread over me
The tabernacle of Thy surpassing peace.
Let the world be lit by Thy full glory,
That we might rejoice and take delight in it.
Hasten, my Beloved, for the time draws nigh,
Bestow Thy grace upon me as in days of yore.

Elazar Azkari put his whole soul into this hymn. The day he wrote it he noted in his diary: "Today my soul has sung its song to God."

Our prayer was led by Ya'akov. His voice imploring God to spread His tabernacle of peace over us was so sweet, and our beings were so stirred, that we felt them light up from within.

I opened my eyes and saw the soldiers of my company. Every one of them was listening. Hanan had put down the hammer and crowbar with which he was working on a tank, to look at us. Sasha came out of his tent and joined us. Zada hummed the melody softly to himself. Ya'akov sang:

"*Hasten, my Beloved, for the time grows nigh...it grows nigh, Beloved, hasten, hasten Thou!*"

So highly strung were our souls in those days that whatever touched them made them tremble.

We finished welcoming the Sabbath and proceeded to the regular evening prayer, saying the *Shema, Hear, O Israel* and the prayer *He Who Spreads a Tabernacle of Peace*, and then silently reciting the *Shmoneh Esreh*. Then we hurried back to our tents to eat the Sabbath meal before the last light faded. Candles were forbidden for reasons of security. Thus our Sabbaths passed in prayers, and in meals, and in singing hymns, and in amity. Most special was our Third Meal, late Saturday afternoon. Refusing to yield to the gathering darkness, we went on discussing the words of the Sages and chanting *Hasidic* melodies to prolong the sanctity of the day, clinging to our Sabbath souls that soon would depart with the Sabbath Queen.

Such were the Sabbaths of our tank battalion in the winter of 1973–74, on the northern Golan Heights between Khan Arnaba and Tel Antar. We derived much comfort from them. They helped us to forget our sorrows and they gave us a sense of purpose and hope. Sometimes we were scrambled in the middle of prayer or eating by a sudden artillery bombardment or a firing order. It didn't faze us. In no time we were in our tanks, loading our guns and preparing to shoot. We did our jobs and returned to our meals and prayers as though we had never left them.

One man alone kept his distance. That is, he did and he didn't. He never lost his weekday look. His eyes were dead even on the Sabbath. His lips remained sealed. When we sang "Dear Friend of my soul," he stood by his tank, aloof. Joining our prayer group for the service, he then returned to it and ate there by himself. No one knew what was the matter with him was. In the *yeshiva* he had been a sociable fellow with a ready smile—a good student, friend, and conversationalist. But we who had been through the war knew it had changed everything. He rebuffed all attempts to approach him. Enveloped in grim silence, he performed his duties like a galley slave.

My heart went out to him. He was one of us, yet we were helpless to lift him out of his abyss. I found myself watching him. Once I thought I glimpsed his eyes light up momentarily. "Tell me about yourself," I said, taking the liberty of putting a hand on his shoulder. He pushed it away. "Leave me alone," he said. "It's too much for me."

Another time, overhearing a conversation at our Third Meal about Faith and Redemption, he snapped angrily, "What in the world are you talking about?"

The Sabbath of the *Torah* portion of *Vayishlach*, which was the second Sabbath of the month of *Kislev*, was like any other. It was a rainy day. Heavy clouds covered the sky. We lingered as usual as the Sabbath drew to an end, before saying the Evening Prayer and the *Havdalah* blessing. Then we gazed at the sky to look for a crack that might let the new moon through. We hadn't yet seen or blessed the moon of *Kislev*—the moon, the Sages said, that was like the People of Israel. For as the moon's light reflects the sun, so does Israel reflect God's presence, and as the moon wanes and waxes, so the destiny of Israel fades and grows bright. Moreover, the People of Israel owe the moon a special debt. This is because on *Rosh Ha-shanah*, the feast of the New Year, when men's souls are weighed in the balance and a prosecuting angel lists the sins of every Jew beneath the heavens, the still darkened moon cannot be found to give testimony. This leaves only the sun—and the *Torah* says: *One witness shall not rise up against a man for any iniquity or for any sin; at the mouth of two witnesses shall the matter be established.* And so, thanks to the moon, the People of Israel are found blameless.

The sky was blanketed by a December fog, through which a pale light, a reflection of a reflection, shone intermittently. The moon was not to be seen. We had vainly searched for it for the last four nights. Tonight marked the start of the tenth day of the month, the last on which the new moon could be blessed. After a while everyone gave up and went to the tanks. "There'll be no moon tonight," they said. "We'll sanctify it next month. Perhaps we'll be home by then."

I refused to give up and went on gazing at the sky. The night was long. Perhaps the clouds would disperse. As I was standing there, Shlomo approached and asked if I would join him for the Fourth Meal. He needed a partner for it and for the *Hasidic* stories he liked to tell then. He was wearing a heavy army coat with several scarves wrapped around it and a balaclava over his face, so that only his smiling eyes were visible. The balaclavas were sent us by schoolchildren whose teachers told them to add a letter to the dear soldiers who watched over them. Sometimes they drew something too—a bright yellow sun in a blue sky or a stick figure with the words "This is me." Attached was a note from The Soldiers Aid Society, requesting us to write back. Not everyone did. Some, touched, responded. Some even wrote the children poems. Others threw the drawings away and kept the balaclava.

Shlomo was the only *Hasid* among us. As a boy he had been brought by his father to the court of the Kloyzenburg *Rebbe* in Netanya, and *Hasidism* pre-occupied him in the *yeshiva* too. There were two customs that he observed more scrupulously than any of us: bathing with hot water on the Sabbath eve and bidding a last farewell to the Sabbath Queen at the Fourth Meal. I don't know whether he knew of a tradition that these things were especially important or whether he had decided that on his own. In any case, he took them seriously.

You may wonder what Jew doesn't bathe before the Sabbath, a point on which the Law is clear. But that winter on the Golan, hot water was at a premium. One Friday afternoon, I remember, Shlomo asked me to accompany him on a search for some. Even after bundling up in our woolen underwear and woolen sweaters and woolen gloves and parkas and ponchos, and clapping a woolen hat on our heads, we still were shivering from the cold. And although we went from unit to unit among the many bivouacked around us, hot water was nowhere to be found. We had all but despaired and were resigned to washing our hair with cold water from the jerry cans like the other men when Shlomo's eyes lit up. Spying a chimney sticking up from an abandoned Syrian army camp, we set out for it. It belonged to an old boiler still connected to a pipe of kerosene and a shower nozzle. By dint of much effort we lit it and waited for it to heat, only to be inundated by a torrent of ice-cold water upon opening the tap. Shlomo refused to accept defeat. We lit the boiler again and waited longer and bathed in water so hot that it left him ecstatically red-faced. Given that ecstasy was a rare commodity in those days, this was nothing to make light of.

Now, Shlomo saw me gazing at the sky and said, "While you're waiting for the moon, come eat David's feast with me."

I went with him. He spread a cloth on some black stones and produced from his pocket a small braided roll, half a tin of sardines, and two plastic forks. We sat in the dark and sang the end-of-the-Sabbath hymn "Fear Not, My Servant Jacob," which has a stanza for every letter of the alphabet and is a fine hymn for not feeling afraid. I followed it with another hymn that we used to sing in my family on Saturday nights in Egyptian Arabic, inviting the Prophet Elijah to visit us. Although Shlomo and I didn't have much in the way of hospitality to offer him, he was still welcome. Then we sang "Happy the man Elijah greets; God bless His people Israel with peace," and sat there thinking about peace.

My friend Shlomo said:

"According to Maimonides, a Sabbath meal must have wine. And since the Fourth Meal is in the Sabbath's honor even though the Sabbath is over, we'll have some wine now too."

I looked at him in amazement. It was all we could do each week to find half a liter of wine for the *Kiddush* and the *Havdalah* blessing—and he now wanted more to toast the Sabbath Queen farewell. Yet off he went and came back with enough for two sips. We said the blessing and drank the wine and he said:

"Now let's talk *Torah*."

I said:

"I've heard there was a custom among the wise Jews of old to tell stories in praise of the People of Israel at the end of the Sabbath. This custom was based on the legend that, every Saturday night, Elijah draws up a list of all Israel's merits during the previous week. Those Jews were learned and knew many things to tell about. We know only what we have seen with our own eyes."

I mentioned something I had seen.

"On the third day of the war, I was waiting at Camp Yiftach for a tank assignment. Next to me was a soldier in a tanker's suit, with a tanker's helmet in his hand. He was dirty and haggard-looking. Since he didn't speak to me, I broke the ice and said, 'Shalom.' 'Shalom,' he answered. I asked where he was from. 'From down south,' he said. 'Ofakim.' He had been in the tank corps a year. 'I'm a driver,' he said. 'I'm waiting for another tank. It will be my fourth. The first three went up in flames. We have to keep fighting.'

"That was all we said to each other."

Shlomo began softly humming a melody of the *Hasidim* of Karlin. It was the song "One Art Thou and One Is Thy Name and None Is Like Thy People Israel." It was said to have been sung by the Karlin in times of trouble.

He said:

"When I was a boy, my father used to take me to the Kloyzenburg *Rebbe* in Netanya. The Kloyzenburger was a great-grandson of that great Jew, Rabbi Haim of Zanz, and a survivor of the camps in which so many died in God's great Holocaust. No man was purer or more holy, and the suffering of Israel was always with him. Once I heard him say, 'I've seen the People of Israel at their worst—and even then their merit surpasses all imagining.' About the verse in Isaiah: *Though your sins be as scarlet, they shall be white as snow*, I heard him say: 'Whatever sins Israel has committed, its years of suffering and exile will bleach them all white.' He said this was the meaning of the statement in Sanhedrin that whenever a wicked Jew is put to death for a capital crime, God's *Shekhinah* cries out, 'Woe to the head! Woe to the hands!' The *Shekhinah* laments because even a wicked man may have had kind thoughts pass through his head or done good deeds with his hands—and if this is so of a Jew who is wicked, how much more is it so of an ordinary Jew who has so much merit to his name. The Rabbi of Kloyzenburg used to say: 'When a *Hasid* goes to see his rabbi, the custom is to give him a slip of paper on which is written the *Hasid*'s name. People think this is so that the rabbi will know whom to pray for. But I tell you that its real purpose is to multiply the merits of the People of Israel. For whenever there is an accusation against a Jew in Heaven, the slip of paper steps forward and says: 'Here is a plain, ordinary Jew—look at how many tribulations he has been through and how much pain he has suffered! He lives among the Gentiles, whose lives are untroubled while his is constantly menaced, and yet he has not changed his Jewish name to pass as one of them. And if the Sages tell us that the People of Israel were delivered from bondage in Egypt because they did not change their names to Egyptian ones, even though they had sunk to the level of the Egyptians and descended through all forty-nine gates of turpitude, how much more deserving must be a simple Jew who turns for help to his rabbi, and this is why he gives him the slip of paper."

I said: "In the *yeshiva*, we sometimes exercised our minds by looking for flaws in the reasoning of Maimonides and then for the flaws in our flaw-finding. Two things come to mind. When we left Camp Yiftach in our tanks on the night after *Yom Kippur* and crossed the bridge over the Jordan, our driver Roni read aloud a passage from Maimonides saying that a man who goes to war mustn't fear. More than that: being afraid, Maimonides says, is like spilling the blood of Israel. I asked myself: how could that be? How could Maimonides tell anyone not to fear war? Think of the night before the breakthrough from Khan Arnaba, when our company was told it would spearhead the attack with mine-detonators tied to the front of our tanks. We all knew it wasn't the cold of the Golan that made our hands shake and our teeth chatter. How could we not have been afraid? That same week we had read in the weekly *Torah* portion how, when he heard that Esau was marching toward him with four hundred men, *Jacob was greatly afraid and distressed*. The Sages took this to mean: *Jacob was greatly afraid*—of being killed. *And distressed*—that he might kill others. And this was despite God's promise to him: *Behold, I am with thee and will keep thee in all places wherever thou may go.* For Jacob feared that his sins might have caused this promise to be revoked. But if we look closely at Maimonides' always impeccable language, we see that he forbade not the fear of war itself, but the yielding to it. A man must not weaken himself and his will to fight by thinking of the horrors of war: it is this that the *Torah* forbids. And the truth is that as soon as we were in combat, we thought only of destroying the enemy's tanks.

"The second thing in Maimonides that bothered me that night

was his saying that whoever goes to war without fear, with a pure mind and a whole heart, will come to no harm and return home safely. How could a philosopher say such a thing? Surely, no one is guaranteed against the Angel of Death. As we were debating this, I remembered a passage in the *Guide To The Perplexed* in which Maimonides writes that he himself was surprised by the philosophical conclusions he came to regarding God's protection of the individual who cleaves to Him with all his heart. And yet even if this is philosophically the case, what individual is so deserving?"

"Sometimes," Shlomo said, "God is merciful even to the undeserving. The individual himself may not know why."

"Yes," I agreed. "That's why David says in his Psalms, *Who remembers us in our low estate, for His mercy endures forever.*"

I was moved to tell Shlomo about God's mercy when our tank was hit. We were still talking when the moon shone through the fog and clouds and we hurried to sanctify it before it could disappear. "As I dance before thee and cannot touch thee," we prayed, "so may none of our enemies touch or harm us or do to us anything at all. May dread and fear befall them! May dread and fear befall them! Let this be a good sign to us and the entire House of Israel! Let this be a good sign to us and to the entire House of Israel! Let this be a good sign to us and to the entire House of Israel!"

We turned to the left and to the right and said to each other, "Peace be upon you." Just then I felt a shadow and heard a faint sound. I turned and saw the soldier who never spoke. He was staring ahead of him without seeing and listening to our conversation without hearing. All at once he said to me in a whisper:

"Were you in Gidi and Roni's tank?"

"Yes," I said.

He whispered:

"Our tank was the last in Nafah quarry to be hit, right after yours. We saw you running when we bailed out. We ran after you. You stopped for a minute by a culvert under the Tapline road and ran some more. We came to it and crawled inside. A few minutes later some Syrians came along and tossed a grenade into it."

He said: "I was the only one who wasn't killed. I was left alone."

Enveloped in silence, he slipped away in the dark. I stood there dumbfounded.

I looked at the moon and saw Dov. We had sanctified the moon of *Tishrei* together, the two of us, in Bayit ve-Gan with the Rabbi of Amshinov.

It was true, I thought. Sometimes God had mercy on the undeserving and shone His light on them. That mercy and that light stayed with you forever. They were a debt you had to repay. There was no getting around it. I thought of the vow I had made while dodging bullets in the wadi. I knew the world would never be the same.

Yes, sometimes God has mercy on the undeserving. And sometimes He descends to His garden, *to the beds of spices to gather lilies*—Sariel and Shmuel and Shaya and Avihu. And Dov. Though we left for the war together.

What was it Rabbi Akiva once said? The Owner of the fig tree knows when it is time to gather His figs.

Who can aim his thoughts as high as those of the Creator of men? In the month of *Elul* we said penitential prayers in my *yeshiva*. Now they echoed in my ears.

> *Who holds in His hand the souls of all that live*
> *And the spirit of each mortal man.*
> *The soul is Yours and the body is Your handiwork.*
> *Spare the work of Your hands.*

> *Lord of all souls, the soul is Yours*
> *But the body is also Your handiwork.*
> *For this it was made, to sanctify Your name in this world.*
> *Master of all worlds, spare the work of Your hands!*

I looked back at the moon. A small cloud had drifted across it. Although it still shone, its light was no longer as bright.

Shlomo put a hand on my shoulder. Softly he began to sing the hymn *"O God Who Hides In Heaven's Vaults,"* which was a favorite of the Rabbi of Kloyzenburg. According to the rabbi's *Hasidim*, he had sung it to himself every Sabbath in the death camps at the time of the Third Meal. His great-grandfather, the *tzaddik* Rabbi Haim of Zanz, sang it then too, in that hour of grace as the Sabbath draws to a close, that hour that is the hour of all hours, his face shining like an angel's.

I stood there in silence. We watched the clouds cover the moon. We bowed to the right and to the left, each toward his friend, and we said:

"Peace be upon you. Peace be upon you. Peace be upon you."

We bowed to the soldier who never spoke and was no longer there and we said:

"Peace be upon you. Peace be upon you. Peace be upon you."

I bowed to the heavens above. I aimed my thoughts at Dov and I said:

"Peace be upon you. Peace be upon you. Peace be upon you."

Glossary

Ahavah ve-Achvah—"Love and Brotherhood"

Arbat haminim—the Four Species used on the *Sukkot* holiday: *lulav* or palm branch; *etrog* or citron; *hadass* or myrtle; and *aravah*, or willow. They are carried during holiday prayers in the synagogue.

Artza—the name of a ship meaning, literally, "to the country/to Israel."

Ashkenazi—The name *Ashkenaz* was applied in the Middle Ages to Jews living along the Rhine River in northern France and western Germany. The center of *Ashkenazi* Jews later spread to Poland-Lithuania and now there are *Ashkenazi* Jews all over the world. The term "*Ashkenaz*" became identified primarily with customs of descendants of European Jews.

Bar Mitzvah—the religious ceremony marking a boy's entry at thirteen into the religious responsibilities of adulthood.

Bava Batra—tractate of the *Talmud*.

Boyan *Hasidim*—a religious sect, see *Hasidim*.

Challah—(plural, *challot*)—Hebrew for "dough offering". Bread used in festive meals on the Sabbath and holidays. There are always two *challot* for each Sabbath meal, to remind Jews of the double portion of *manna* they received on Fridays in the desert so they would not have to gather food on the Sabbath.

Elul—last month of the Hebrew calendar, (usually August, beginning of September), a time of prayer and repentence in preparation for *Rosh Ha-shanah*, the Jewish New Year.

Etrog—a citron, used on the festival of *Sukkot*.

Gefilte fish—fish that has been filleted, the bones removed, and often cooked with breadcrumbs and carrots to give it a sweetish taste. A delicacy often made with carp, left to set and gel; it is eaten cold, often with horseradish.

Halacha, halachic—("the way/path")—collectively, the laws and ordinances of Judaism.

Hallel—a recitation of Psalms (113–118) recited on holidays and *Rosh Hodesh* (the New Moon which marks the beginning of the new month).

Hanukkah—("dedication") Eight-day celebration commemorating the victory of the Maccabees over the Greek forces which occupied the land of Israel during part of the Second Temple period.

Hasid, Hasidim—members of the Jewish sect of *Hasidism*, a vibrant religious and social movement founded by Israel Ba'al Shem Tov (1699–1761) in Volhynia and Podolia. It taught that all were equal before the Almighty (the ignorant no less honored than the learned), that purity of heart was superior to study, and that devotion to prayer and the commandments was to be encouraged but ascetic practices eschewed. The movement spread rapidly throughout Eastern Europe in the 18th century. There are many offshoots, each centered around a charismatic leader, including Gerer, Habad (Lubavitch), Satmar and may others.

Havdalah—ceremony marking the end of the Sabbath. It consists of blessings over wine, spices, and a candle, and the main blessing, which refers to the distinction between holy and profane.

Heshvan—second month of the Jewish calendar, usually falling around October/November.

Ima—Hebrew for "mother".

Ketubot—tractate of the *Talmud* dealing with the laws of marriage and women.

Kibbutznik—member of a *kibbutz*, a communal farming settlement of which there are many in Israel, often with a population the size of a village or town.

Kiddush—blessing over wine, said on the Sabbath and Festivals at the evening and mid-day meals.

Kiddush Levanna—The Sanctification of the New Moon, recited at the first appearance of the New Moon, normally after the close of Shabbat. A central feature is when those at prayer wish their neighbors "Peace unto you" three times. *Kiddush Levanna* has deep symbolic significance, signally the "rebirth" of hope for the Jewish people after a decline, and Cabbalistic significance, revealing the orderly functioning of the Universe.

Kislev—third month of the Jewish calendar, falling around December.

Lulav—(palm branch) used ritually, see *Arbat Haminim*.

Magen David—"Star of David", Jewish symbol and common motif for decoration and religious artifacts.

Maharal—Rabbi Judah Loew ben Bezalel, also known as the *Maharal*, c. 1525–1609. An outstanding Talmudic scholar and Kabbalist. Rabbi in Prague and a recognized leader of Ashkenazi Jewry, many legends grew up around him, and in the late 18th century, the tale of the Golem was associated with him as well.

Maimonides—Rabbi Moshe ben Maimon (1135–1204), also known as the *Rambam*, perhaps the greatest of the medieval Jewish philosophers. Born in Spain, he fled persecution there, and eventually settled in Egypt, where he was the chief physician to the Caliph. His principal works include his codification of Jewish Law, the *Mishneh Torah*, and his principal philosophic work, *The Guide to the Perplexed*.

Matzah—(plural: *Matzot*)—unleavened bread, used as the symbol and staple food for *Pesach* (Passover) referred to in the Bible as the "bread of affliction"—indicating the time of the Israelite slavery in Egypt.

Mezuzah—("doorpost")—a case attached to the doorposts of houses, containing a scroll with passages of scripture written on it.

Minyan—a Jewish prayer quorum requiring a minimum of ten adult males.

Mishnah—Legal codification containing the core of the Oral Law. It was edited by Rabbi Judah HaNasi on the basis of previous collections and was issued around the end of the second/beginning of the third centuries.

Mishneh Torah, written by Maimonides. He codified therein the entire body of Jewish law. This was the product of years of work and the first systematic codification of the entire corpus of Jewish law ever written. Unlike all of the *Rambam's* other works, the Mishneh Torah was written in Hebrew and was intended to provide the average Jew with access to the body of Jewish law. It is still used daily by students.

Mitnaggedim (Heb. "opponents"): Opponents of the *Hasidic* movement.

Mitzvah—(plural: *mitzvoth*)—loosely, a "good deed" but it refers to the 613 commandments (positive and negative) as found in the *Torah*, the Pentateuch.

Pesach—("Passover") First of the three festivals of pilgrimage to Jerusalem, it is observed for seven days in the spring and commemorates the Exodus from Egypt. On the eve of the festival all leavened foods are cleared from the home and it is prohibited to eat or possess such foods for the duration of the festival, during which only unleavened bread—*matzah*—is consumed.

Phylacteries, see *tefillin*.

Piercers—pointy rounds that go straight into a tank, whereas **squash heads** blow it up without penetrating. **H.E.S.H.**—**High Explosive Squash Head**: rather than relying on the speed of the round achieving a penetrating blow, it flies slower but is far heavier.

Prayer group, see *Minyan*.

Purim—("Drawn Lots")—The Festival of Purim commemorates and celebrates the story told in the Biblical Book of Esther, which tells of the delivery of the Jews from the threat of total destruction at the hands of Haman, principal advisor to King Ahaseurus of Persia.

Rabbi Akiva—Akiva Ben Joseph; c. 50–135 C.E. According to legend, he was of humble origin and remained uneducated until the age of 40, when, with the assistance and encouragement of his wife Rachel, he devoted himself to learning. When the Roman government prohibited the study of the Law, Akiva ignored the decree. He was arrested as a rebel and ultimately executed at Caesarea. No rabbi of the *Talmudic* period made a more profound impression on Jewish history and on the imagination of the Jewish people.

Rabbenu Tam—("our perfect master"): Jacob Ben Meir Tam c. 1100–1171, grandson of *Rashi*. He was the outstanding rabbinical authority of his day, and the leading figure of the school of *Talmudic* analysis known as *Tosafot*.

Rabbi Haninah ben Teradyon—(flourished 2nd century), headed a famous school, Siknin, in Galilee. He publicly opposed the Hadrianic decree forbidding religious teaching, and for that was wrapped in a *Torah* scroll and burned. (His daughter, Bruriah, became the wife of Rabbi Meir).

Rabbi Isaac Ben Solomon Luria—(1534–1572)—in abbreviation, the "Ari". He was a renowned kabbalist, born in Jerusalem, educated in Egypt, and lived in Safed from 1570, renowned for his ascetic life and saintly character. His teachings, received by his disciples orally, were posthumously recorded.

Rabbi Meir Baal HaNess—("Rabbi Meir the Miracle Worker"), the appellation is ascribed to the Mishnaic authority Rabbi Meir on account of miracles attributed to him in Aggadic literature.

Rashi—Rabbi Solomon Yitzhaki (1040–1105): Great French rabbinical scholar. A leading *halachic* authority of his time, his greatest contributions to Jewish learning are his remarkably lucid commentaries on the Bible and the Babylonian *Talmud*. They remain the most popular commentaries on these works to this very day.

Rebbe—Yiddish form of 'rabbi', applied generally to a teacher; also to a *Hasidic* rabbi.

Rosh Ha-shanah—the Jewish New Year, starting with the month of *Tishrei* (around September).

Sephardi—someone originating from 'Sepharad' the Hebrew name for Spain. The name *Sephardi* was given to the Jews of Spain, and to their descendents, who eventually dispersed primarily to North Africa, the Middle East and Southern Europe. In modern times, the term has come to denote all North African Jews, as well as those from the communities in Egypt, Syria, Iraq, Iran, the Balkans, Turkey—and loosely—all non-*Ashkenazi* Jews.

Seven Species—pomegranate, vine, olive, date palm, wheat, barley and fig. See *Shivat Haminim*

Sha'ar ha-shamayim—the "Gates of Heaven".

Shabbat—the Sabbath, the seventh day of the week, which is the biblically ordained holy day of rest.

Shavuot—the feast of Pentecost, exactly seven weeks after Passover.

Shekhinah—the divine Presence, (from "to dwell").

Shema—abbreviation for *Shema Yisrael*, "Hear O Israel, the Lord is our God, the Lord is one", (Deut. 6:4), Judaism's profession of faith, proclaiming the absolute unity of God, and recited twice in daily worship—in the evening and in the morning. Countless Jewish martyrs met their death while reciting this prayer.

Shmoneh Esreh—("The Eighteen Benedictions")—which constitute the central part of the three daily prayers.

Shulhan Aruch—("The Prepared Table")—the authoritative code of Jewish Law written by Rabbi Joseph Caro (1488–1575).

Shivat Haminim—"The Seven Species," the biblical 'seven agricultural products'—pomegranate, vine, olive, date palm, wheat, barley and fig.

Shofar—ram's horn. Biblical law prescribes its sounding for the memorial blowing on the New Year (*Rosh Ha-shanah*), where it is intended as a clarion call to repentance and as a reminder of the *Akedah*—the Sacrifice of Isaac.

Shtreimels—wide fur-rimmed hats worn by *Hasidic* Jews, imitative of the garb worn by medieval Polish aristocracy.

Squash noses—part of a tank's arsenal of ammunition, causing damage primarily because of its exploding head.

Sukkah—("Tabernacle")—a temporary makeshift dwelling built for eating and sleeping in on the Festival of *Sukkot*, which occurs in the fall (September/October).

Sukkot—("Tabernacles") is one of the three pilgrim festivals. It occurs in the fall and lasts for seven days. It is celebrated by taking the *Arbat Haminim* (see above) and by eating and sleeping in the *Sukkah*.

Talmud—Hebrew for "teaching," the name applied to both the Babylonian *Talmud* and the Palestinian *Talmud*. It is the collected records of academic discussion and case law by generations of scholars during several centuries after 200 C.E. and is also referred to as the *Gemara*. The term *Talmud* may also refer to the *Mishnah*, together with the *Gemara*. Study of the *Talmud* constitutes the largest part of *Yeshiva* studies.

Talmud Torah—Jewish traditional school for young boys devoted primarily to the study of the *Talmud* and rabbinic literature. It is a preparation for *yeshiva*.

Tanker—a generic term that refers to all who serve in tanks.

Tefillin—Phylacteries, or prayer boxes, strapped to the head and arm, worn during the daily *Shacharit*, or morning prayers, but not on holidays or the Sabbath. They are the sign of the covenant between God and His people.

Third Meal, or *Seudah Shlishit*—the meal traditionally eaten just before the conclusion of the Sabbath, the first two being the meal on the Sabbath eve, and lunch on Sabbath.

Tikvatenu—("our hope") **Athletic Club**—a national network of community centers for youth.

Tishrei—first month of the Jewish calendar, usually falling around September/October.

Torah—the Pentateuch: the Five Books of Moses, constituting the first section of the Bible.

Tzaddik—("righteous man"), title given to a person noted for outstanding faith and piety. The concept of the *tzaddik* gained great significance in *Hasidism*.

Tzion—Hebrew form of the man's name, Zion.

Tzizit—("fringes")—The Bible commands the wearing of *Tzizit* (Numbers 15:37–41) on the four corners of garments for all males.

Yarmulka—skullcap, worn by observant Jewish men and boys.

Yeshiva—Jewish traditional school devoted primarily to the study of the *Talmud* and rabbinic literature.

Yoma—tractate of the *Talmud*.

Yom Kippur—the Day of Atonement, which is the holiest day in the Jewish calendar, the tenth of *Tishrei*. It is the day on which Jews beg forgiveness for their transgressions against God and man.

About the author

Haim Sabato

Haim Sabato, born in Cairo, Egypt, in 1952, descends from a long line of rabbis from Aleppo, Syria. His family lived in Egypt for two generations, before moving to Israel when he was five. He served in the tank corps in the 1973 Yom Kippur War, and teaches in a Yeshiva near Jerusalem, which he co-founded.

Sabato's first novel, *Emet Me'Eretz Titzmach,* appeared in 1997. His second novel, *Tiyum Kavanot,* "Adjusting Sights," was awarded the prestigious Sapir Prize for Literature in 2000 and the Sadeh Prize for Literature in 2002.

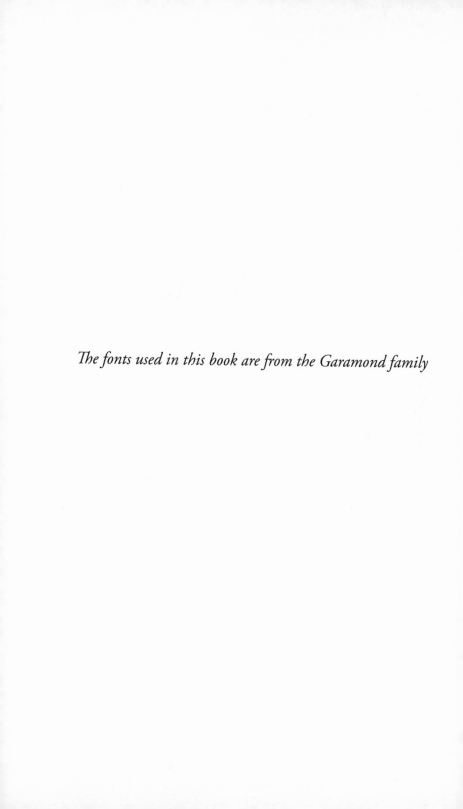

The fonts used in this book are from the Garamond family

The Toby Press publishes fine fiction,
available at fine bookstores everywhere. For more information,
please contact *The* Toby Press at www.tobypress.com